THE SOLITUDE OF THOMAS CAVE

THE SOLITUDE OF THOMAS CAVE

GEORGINA HARDING

BLOOMSBURY

Published by Bloomsbury USA, New York
Distributed to the trade by Holtzbrinck Publishers

All papers used by Bloomsbury USA are natural, recyclable products made from wood grown in well-managed forests. The manufacturing processes conform to the environmental regulations of the country of origin.

Library of Congress Cataloging-in-Publication Data has been applied for.

ISBN-10 1-59691-272-3
ISBN-13 978-1-59691-272-4

First U.S. Edition 2007

1 3 5 7 9 10 8 6 4 2

Typeset by Hewer Text UK Ltd, Edinburgh
Printed in the United States of America by Quebecor World Fairfield

To Nell and Tom

THE NARRATIVE
OF THOMAS GOODLARD

Related on the Suffolk coast, one evening of June 1640

1

I SHALL NOT FORGET the sight of him as we left, that
picture stays strong with me: his figure still and straight on
the wide shore, the land huge and bare about him, the
snowy dip of the valley at his back, the mountains on either
side, twin peaks they were of seeming identical height, rising
steep and smooth and streaked with grey as if in some strange
reversal the rock were ashes that had been poured down on
to the snow from heaven; the sea a darkened pewter and
having that sluggishness to its movement that comes when it
is heavy with the beginnings of ice. In all God's Earth, from
the tip of Africa to the Indies or the wide Pacific, a man
might never see a sight so lonely.

Other times there would have been talk in the boat as we
rowed out to the ship where it lay at anchor. Some way to
go, as the bay there is wide and shallow, the boat crammed
with men, with the last of us and the last bits of stuff that we
must take with us, the *Heartsease* already laden heavy for the
voyage home, with its weight of whalebone and sea-horse

tusks and one hundred and fifty tons of whale oil from what had been a slow but at the end bountiful season; in other times there would have been a chorus of talk rich as you might hear on land in an inn after market day, richer, the resonant talk of men with hard and perilous work done, money made, going home. You know how it is at times like that: the jokes run fast and the long voyage south seems but a spin before the breeze.

This day there was scarce a sound to be heard. Not even William Sherwyn the carpenter uttered a word, and he was ever a talker, though once I think I caught his eye and saw his lips begin to move and then to clip shut again. Juan or John Ezkarra who was a Biscayan tried to whistle one of his country's yearning tunes but the notes came thin and pained in that frigid air and after a couple of phrases he relinquished the effort. From then on there was only the dip of the oars in the slow water. That, and as we neared the *Heartsease*, the creak of the ship herself as she moved, the thresh of ropes as they were caught in the wind, the to and fro of sailors that were beginning to be busy in the rigging and on the deck. Our boat banged against the ship's side, we stowed the oars, tied in, and one by one and slow as seals that lumber on to land we made the climb on board, each man pulling up his feet after him as if they might be heavy as lead, looking back when he reached the deck and Captain Marmaduke standing there, following the Captain's gaze and turning to see the land again and make out through narrowed lids the still figure at the edge of the bay. Any person that observed in ignorance might have said from our faces that it was we who were the men set to serve a sentence, that it was any one of us, not he ashore, that looked on this pale day with the dread prospect of darkness before him and the knowledge that he might never again see the green sweep of his native coast.

And all that time it seemed to me that he only stood and watched. I went up to the masthead as we set sail, as the light north-easterly picked up and gently bore us away. I saw him standing still as a post or a tree in a land where there were no trees, watched as he thinned and faded, and the land about him looked so huge and cold and stony still you had not believed a single man might walk upon it.

I never thought to see Thomas Cave alive again.

We tacked to and fro amongst the incoming ice and made our slow way down the great fjord, a luminous streak in the sky like mother-of-pearl showing where the expanse of the Greenland seas opened before us. At the last sight of the bay, Marmaduke had a cannon fired. The noise of the shot was so big in the emptiness that I was sure that it must have shaken him there, shaken too the last of the birds from the rocks come to dive and wheel and scream like dervishes about him.

Carnock did not speak save for the necessary, not a human word out of him that day, nor most of the next. He knew that eyes were on him: for asking the question, making the challenge, pushing the man into what he had done. Carnock was never one who knew when to stop.

Only Ezkarra the Biscayan spoke to him direct. A dark man with dark rings beneath his eyes like he had overworked them, a harpooneer with more knowledge of whales than any other man aboard. 'It is not for you he does this, even though he makes you think that way.'

'How can you say that?' says Carnock, sullen in his responsibility. 'You were there. You heard it.'

'I hear his words, but I am sitting away from you, I can see his face. He had the will on him to escape you all. I see that. I see that he is like a whale that must make its run to the ice.'

'Don't talk in riddles, man. What do you mean?'

'I mean that he goes to hide himself in the ice. His instinct tells him that of all the places in the world the ice is safest if it is man that he wants to escape, that in the ice he is out of reach.'

'He made a boast, the drink took him, that's all. There was a devil of a mood in him that night, you all saw. And he was too proud to go back on his word once he'd spoken it. He's never a man of many words, Cave, but by God when he speaks 'em he means to hold to 'em. He's a stubborn proud man.'

'It is possible, Mister Carnock.' Ezkarra's voice was smooth as oil on water. 'But it is possible that he does it anyway. I think that he is only looking for a cause.'

Those light nights get to men. I knew that by then. I had learnt much over that first northern summer. You get dizzy with the light, as if all the time you were a little drunk. Cave

6

got reckless with it. No doubt he wasn't the first and he won't be the last: mild, God-fearing men driven reckless out there, men not in their right world as if the Lord had never meant them to go there, out of reach of all they were born to, that gives them proportion, all that is blessed by God and human-size, where day runs into night and the works of man are hellish and the beasts so monstrous that the object of the hunt is bigger than any creature should rightly be.

There had been no whales for some days. I remember well the whole sequence of events. We had not seen a whale nor heard the sound of one since the fog had come in more than a week earlier, rolling up before the south wind to stand and intensify in the bay. For days we had seen no more than the looming shapes of the cookery, the tents and the weird grey outlines of all the hoists and coppers and paraphernalia with which the oil was rendered, and amongst these, the looming forms of other men that sometimes we took to be bears and the forms of rocks that we took to be men. Nothing I have seen is so disorienting as that summer fog, disorienting as much in the mental as in the visual sense since there is no distinguishing any one of twenty-four hours, no time to be estimated by position of sun or planet nor by any alteration of light whatsoever. In conditions such as that it is not uncommon for a man to look up from his work in which he has been absorbed for some hours' monotony, to start and look about him in bewilderment, and look to his companions and ask if it be day or night, and they cannot tell him and it becomes a subject of debate.

After days such as those I cannot describe the beauty of a change of weather. A movement of moisture, a shift of air that

7

broke it into separate strands of opacity and translucence. A breath of air down our necks that made us shiver. We looked up to the forgotten sky and the fog had become no more than a fine veil that all of a sudden was drawn away, and the mountains that had ceased for us to exist were revealed sharp as knives with that extraordinary blue distance above them, and then we looked about us and saw the shore where we had been used to groping like blind men, the strewn ugliness of our settlement, the machinery and the tents and the barrels of oil, and here and there in the discoloured and greasy water of the shallows the putrid remnants of all the great beasts we had caught since the start of the season, stripped of what remained of their flesh through the days of fog by an eerie white seethe of seabirds. The clean breeze pushed on and within a day had cleared the bay before us free of all ice, leaving the water open and dark as a lake inviting pleasure boats upon it. And there was not a whale in sight.

At once the harpooneers set out, five or six gangs in the whaleboats, to see what hunting might be found along the coast. We had loitered about so long that there was impatience amongst all of us for action. Marmaduke himself took some men with him inland. He said he meant to explore and to see if he could climb one of the peaks behind the bay; see what might be seen from there, signs of whales, of ice far out, of other ships that might have found the quarry. Up there, if God were willing, the ascent easy and the sky clear, he would have a view far across and down the fjord to the open sea, a view along the shore in both directions and one inland of regions where no man of our knowing had ever yet penetrated.

The rest of us were left to kick our heels under the command of the Mate Carnock. I hardly wished that but as the youngest of the crew I did not have the choice. I recall that I envied the men who set off with the Captain, jealous of their adventure and also, as I think now but would not have put it then, that they would for the duration of their expedition have escaped the restless ocean, that they would have the touch of soil and whatever greenness the land offered beneath their feet. It was just at that moment that Thomas Cave came by, and stood there by me, and he saw what was in my mind though the two of us had exchanged scarce more than a word before that day.

'You'll get your chance,' he said.

And I, watching them go up off the rocky shore and along the valley: 'There's grass there, see, and flowers, on the slope that faces the sun.'

'Aye, boy, it's happy as a meadow, isn't it? And who'd have thought it here? And do you know, if you look, you'll find tiny wizened trees that stand no more than two inches high?'

'They'll have the hay in by now at home,' I said, 'dry and stacked.'

So he asked me where my home was and I told him. In Suffolk, inland, in the valley of the Alde. And I told him the name of my village even, but said the word for myself only in my moment's homesickness, that I might speak it aloud and hear its familiarity, never suspecting that he should know of it.

At that he looked at me hard, and for the first time I felt the clarity of those pale eyes of his that were like a fine December sky. He looked, and a slow smile broke on his face so that he seemed quite unlike his former self. I had thought him a stern and watchful man; I did not expect to see such softness in him.

'Why, that's a mere handful of miles from my own home!'

And I said how I had travelled from there to the sea, two days it took and it was the only journey that I had made, and he nodded at the names of the places I had passed through as he knew them also, and all the time he smiled, so widely that it warmed me, and put a hand to my shoulder, and that was warm too.

'A Suffolk lad,' he said. 'I had the thought of it. I thought some time ago that I might have heard it in your voice but doubted, I had been away so long, thought that there was something in you that I knew and now I see it's that, and it's not the name alone that we bear in common, common enough a name as it is. So what brought you here of all places, Thomas, what brought you to this God-lorn spot?'

'My cousin's ship brought me to Hull and there I found a place on this one. To try the whaling.'

'Your cousin's ship?'

'I had been sent to my cousin who worked a ship out of Aldborow. There were too many of us, you see, to stay at home.'

'And did you want that?'

'Oh, yes and no, sir. I mean that I miss my home and all but it's a wonder to be here, isn't it?'

'What's a wonder?'

'Why, the place. The adventure. The difference of it. It's all so very different.'

'Ah, Thomas, Tom, do they call you Tom? And so you like adventure? And no doubt you've heard of Eldorado?'

'Who's Eldorado?'

Thomas Cave laughed. He laughed as if he had not done so in years. He was a tall, gaunt man, no longer young, and when he laughed like that he hollowed out and bent over and went on till he coughed, and put a hand on my shoulder to straighten himself so that I saw that his eyes brimmed with tears.

'It's a place, Tom, and no one knows where it is. And a man might put it before anything else, and go in search of it, and find himself instead in a land of ice.'

And again he laughed, but I heard a harshness there that made me ill at ease, and shy, as I did not know what cause he had to laugh so hard at me.

I did not like to say then that I still did not understand what he spoke. Yet as we became friends in the weeks that followed he spoke of it again as if it was often in his mind, some meaning or reflection in the word that threw a glow of yellow sunlight across the ice about us: that land of gold that the Spaniards have a name for but have never found, that Raleigh had sought and, though we did not know it, was seeking again those very days as we worked there in the cold, and for which in the end he was to lose first his son and then his life. It came clear to me in time that for Thomas Cave also Eldorado had been a dream and that the irony that stung me in his laughter was no more than the irony with which he had come to regard his own youth, his lust for adventure, his coming to sea at all.

But I run ahead. This came later. My knowledge and my

friendship for the man came later. I was meaning to speak of this one day, this one day and the night when the wager was made.

We talked and watched until the exploration party was quite lost from view, and then we heard the calls of the others who had remained on the shore. They had sighted on the rocks about the point a group of seals and wanted the hunting of them, a last chance for it was late in the season and the great multitude by now had reared their young and gone. So we went and joined them and set out swiftly in the one boat that was left to us – if the harpooneers were to find no whales, we thought, here at least God's bounty might offer us some small opportunity of profit. Yet it was hardly a herd at all, so small a number of individuals that would not yield a caskful of oil. We satisfied ourselves with killing one for our dinner and then we had some sport. There were some pups among them and three of the men took one of these and flayed it alive as it was, and then threw it back into the surf for a prank, and it swam about in its red suit and writhed and twisted as its companions came frisking and barking about it. You cannot imagine if you have not seen it, how strong a seal may be, so strong in muscle and so tenacious of life that it will swim unto the very last. We watched until the commotion was done, and then we went back and built a fire to cook by, and waited for our shipmates to return from their exploration.

I think that we all felt the better for that hunt, our fretful spirits exercised, released after the pent days of fog – all of us but Cave that is, who for some reason I did not then know, whether someone had spoken to him amiss or whether something else untoward had occurred, bore a scowl set deep on his face all the rest of that evening, a blackness, I know now, that was brewing in him, that was to come out later beside the fire.

It must have been near midnight though the sun still threw its low light across the mountains and the sea. We had built this great fire on the strand and sat close about it because of the coldness of the air. We had eaten of the fresh meat, a fatty meat but tasty, the liver in particular having a fine flavour, and in celebration of the turn in weather and the hope of a corresponding turn in the fortune of the season, we had broken open a new cask of brandy and it loosened the men's tongues so that if they had been in a tavern and enclosed with walls and ceilings you would not have heard yourself think for the noise.

William Sherwyn in particular ran with stories. He was an oddity, Sherwyn, odd to find him at sea. He might as easily have plied his trade anywhere, in a workshop with a street outside and all kinds of folk and dogs and boys coming in and out stepping through the sawdust on the floor. But he had an eye for strange things and marvels; I guess that was what set him on the move. He packed up his chest of tools and left whatever town it was and took ship and came to see the world, and he had this knack of gathering curiosities to him wherever he went, even when we had visited the very same place as himself and found only the common and the ordinary. In Bergen I recall he had seen the work of a master clockmaker from Italy, a clock fitted into the form of a magnificent castle with eighteen bells which chimed to bring in the hour. And when the first stroke came, two doors would open, and two angel sentries spring up and blow on their heavenly clarions, and through the opening would enter a form that seemed to be the actual living Christ, and He would stretch out His hands and invite all onlookers to come to Him, the form of His humanity so convincing that women in the crowd were seen to cry with joy at the miracle of His coming. There was debate amongst us on that. Only clockwork, someone said, a mechanical marvel. A work of illusion, said another, the Italians had a famous talent for illusions. All a gross exaggeration, said Carnock, the women must have been either witless or drunk to be so moved; if only he had been present he would have seen through whatever device it was in an instant.

He did not tolerate others easily, Mister Carnock. William was a harmless fellow, a shy one at heart I think who talked to fill a silence or to entertain and never meant to upset a soul. Yet more than once I saw Carnock take issue with him on the accuracy of his tales. I saw no need for that, nor did any other of us. I believed that the things he told us were substantially true, that he did indeed have an exceptional eye and ear for the wondrous, yet that is not to say that I did not at times suspect that his marvels had grown at the least a little more marvellous in the telling.

It was another story of William's that night that set off the wager. It all came out in passing, as such things do. Neither William nor any one of us might have predicted the consequences of what he was to say, which was the mention only of how he had met in Amsterdam a Dutchman who claimed to have lived an entire year on Jan Mayen – this was an island much frequented by the whalers of that nation and some distance to the south of where we were. And this was a story which I believe William told very straight. Indeed, I think he needed no embellishment for the plain facts of it were strange enough to catch the mind.

It would appear that the crew of this Dutchman's whaleboat had been left accidentally stranded at the end of a late season, unable to rejoin the ship as it escaped the fast-closing ice, and they had no choice but to upturn the boat and make a house out of it and try to endure there through the dark months of winter, contriving a stove somehow and hunting down whatever scarce game was to be found, but meagrely, until one by one they succumbed to scurvy and the body of each was disposed of in turn, laid out on the frozen soil and covered over with rocks as was the sailor's common way of burial in those places, or wedged into some crevice inaccessible to scavenging bears, until there remained only this single man, an exceptionally wiry and determined fellow who would not stop for the scurvy to take hold but sought endlessly all the long spring for fresh food, for bear and game and the bitter but life-saving grasses that were at last uncovered beneath the snow. When he was found by a returning whaler he was barely alive, barely able to drag out from beneath the boat the body of the last of his companions and lay it wrapped tight in sailcloth on the beach. And at that season's end they had brought him home and now he would not go back to sea but lived raggedly by the portside in Amsterdam, making his home again, but not such a cold one, in a capsized boat, and supported by those to whom he told his tale so that he need never seek out a hunk of bread or a drink again.

Carnock laughed at that point, a lone hard laugh. 'And what did you give him for his fine tale?'

William looked about, surprised at the intervention. 'What I could. It's not so far off a possibility that I could not imagine such a thing might befall to myself, to any one of us here. Of course I gave him something.'

'God's Truth, William, I'll wager you did, and every guilder of it was tricked out of you. You of all men might have seen through such a fraud,' said Carnock, with that scornful way he had that could make even the least criticism he spoke come across like an insult. How he survived so long as Mate, with that aggressive manner and the power he had over us, sometimes amazed me, that he was not found some day beaten in an alley round the back of some harbour or simply gone overboard in the night.

'What do you mean by that?' William came back, and Carnock did not see fit to stop there.

'I had thought, William Sherwyn, that a man such as yourself was especially well placed to recognise the invention that goes into the telling of tales.'

At that William bridled. Like many talkers, he was a nervous man, slight and quick, precise with his hands and his tools, and he had a ginger temper to him. I would not have given much for his chances against a man the size of Carnock if it had come to a fight. Yet it did not come to that for Cave intervened, intervened with a quiet authority that directed all attention on to him and let William shrink back small and soon forgotten.

'I have met this fellow myself, heard him talk. I am convinced of the truth of his story.' Cave's voice came through strong, all the richer for being not too often wasted.

Carnock turned to find Cave's face across the fire. 'What are you saying, man? You have experience of these regions. You know sure well as I do that no man of flesh and blood lives a winter this far north.'

'And yet it is my conviction that he spoke the truth. I heard the details of his story and I saw the look in his eyes.'

'Then he's a fine actor and a finer liar than our friend William here. Because any fool knows that what he says is an impossibility.'

'Not at all.' Cave spoke calmly against the Mate's swagger. That calm in his voice gave it power, and I was drawn to it and forgot all else as it ran on into philosophy in that stark midnight light. I remember the eeriness of the light and the coolness of his voice: 'A man never knows what is or is not possible until he has tried it.'

'Some things a man is wise enough not to try.'

'Men who think like that gain no wisdom. They have beliefs, prejudices, superstitions; they may think they have certainty but they have no wisdom. Wisdom lies in finding out for yourself.'

Carnock was losing his depth. 'Say what you like, any man left a winter up here would be mad by Christmas and dead by New Year. Mad from the cold and the dark and the lights in the sky, dead from scurvy and starvation.'

'Not if he is strong and free from fear. If he cleanses

17

himself of superstition. If he is a practical man, if he has reason and self-discipline, and if he has God's help and a little luck.' There was something elevated about the way Cave spoke, as if he knew something we did not, like the priest in the pulpit with the ignorant populace beneath him. Carnock did not like to be spoken to in such a way.

'In God's Name then, do it yourself.'

'I might.'

'You *might*?' The scorn in his word cracked the air. 'Hear that, lads? Our Mister Cave says he *might* spend a winter here.'

Every one of us fell still then. Slowly chat and movement had been dying down as all the rest of them came to take notice of the argument. Now in the pause not a man moved and you could hear the burning of the fire before us. The flames were bright, the smoke carried the fishy taint of blubber. Even on a summer's night we each of us knew inside the fear we had of those lands. Even on the brightest morning when the sun's rays came hot through the thin air and burned our faces and we worked in our undershirts, we had the sense that this was not a place that God had made for man, that no man surely was meant in His plan to set foot on its land or sail its seas, that we were overbold to come there and hunt in the way that we did. In this place the very days did not have the form God had given them in the habitable regions, nor the seasons either, it being possible to experience the most extreme cold and blizzard even at the height of August; in its heavens we saw weird apparitions and lights that were not meant for our eyes, and in its sea we saw extraordinary beasts akin to the creatures of myth. Recognising that, we were touched with dread even when the sun shone, and each day we spent there in the North came to seem a transgression. To suggest remaining an entire year seemed the utmost temptation of fate.

Only Thomas Cave showed no awe of the place. His voice ran on into our silence, easy as if he spoke not there but on some mild English shore.

'Yes, I say that, with God's help, I could spend a winter here.' And he looked about him, at the pale night, the mountains, the slatey sea of the bay with the *Heartsease* at anchor.

'You'll die a fool.'

'Better than living a fool,' said Cave, and I believe that the sting in his words was meant as much for himself as for Carnock but Carnock of course did not see it that way.

'Do it then, Devil take you. What do you say, lads? We'll leave him ship's stores, musket, powder, all he thinks he might need. And when we come back next year we'll see if he's still warm.'

And so the wager was made. He drew us in, Carnock, for we all were sided with him and against Cave on the one matter of which we were sure: that no mortal man might live out the winter there. From one to the other of us he looked, and said, you'd bet it wasn't possible, wouldn't you? And of course we meant that it was an impossibility but we did not intend that anyone should take up the bet. It was an argument, theoretical, fed by the drink and the lightness of the night, no more. And yet there, with the sun bleeding low over the horizon and the fire warm on our faces, it took on practical reality. Ten of us, ten pounds each man, a hundred pounds in all.

The day before we sailed was one of those bright ones when the atmosphere alone is sharp enough to etch itself on the senses and the memory. No need for that, since I was already tight with anticipation of our parting. In those few weeks I had come to admire Cave more than any man, more even than Marmaduke, not for any heroics but for the bare dignity in him and the calm with which he looked ahead. I think that I was moved the more because of our common past which gave me sight of the humanness of him; but for that it is possible that I might have taken his impassivity for hardness and judged him without warmth of either flesh or heart.

We took a short walk that last day, took what brief time as other things allowed. Cave had sought me out. I and some others had helped him stow the provisions the Captain had allotted him for the winter in the cabin that was to be his home, and a generous enough supply it was: hogsheads of oatmeal and barley, casks of beer and oil, breads, bacon and cheeses, salt, brandy, spices, all that the ship could spare to be left behind, such a variety of things and such a quantity that the narrow cabin came to resemble nothing so much as a grocery shop. And when all was done, and the three muskets that he was to be left with and sufficient powder also safely and dryly put away, he singled me out and had me come with him.

We walked up the back of the beach to a place in the

valley where there was a small dark tarn round and brown as a cow's eye. Earlier I had seen snipe there, surprised them from the surrounding bog and known them in the instant by their sudden zigzag flight, but the birds had gone.

'Flown south,' Cave said.

'Jonas Watson says they are the same birds we see at home, that they come here as we do only for the summer.'

'Could be.'

'Reckon it gets too cold for them soon. They'd die of cold.'

And as I spoke the thought stabbed me like a snipe's curved beak, and I wished that I had not said the words.

The brook that ran down from the tarn burbled faintly, its water and its little cascades soon to be silenced beneath a glassy casing of ice. So silent it was there, heavy with the intense quiet of inland, the calls of gulls and of men loading ship carrying now and then wavering and thin from the sea's edge.

Cave had planned what he would say.

'I'll have you take my share, boy. I have written it over for you, given my paper to the Captain. My portion of the sale of the oil and the whalebone. Also of the unicorn's horn. The value of that is hard to tell but, believe me, it is great. It is inestimably rare, said to be a most powerful antidote to poisons though of course I have no experience, no proof of that. I have heard that such a horn may trade for twenty times its weight in gold. See that the Captain deals fair and gives you all that is due to me.'

His was the largest share of this since it was he who had found the skull, on the strand line of a narrow beach beyond

21

the mountain north of our bay, the skull of a strange beast with this one huge whorled shaft, a full eight foot long, projecting from it.

'No, sir,' I said, unable to admit this favour from the man whose fate seemed so inevitable before me. 'I will not take it. I will hold it for you.'

'Take it, Tom. Invest the money well. You are young. You may use it to build a future. A few good voyages and you may yet have your own ship, you never know, or if you choose, a place on land.'

'Till next season, I will hold it.'

'No. You will take it for your own.'

I gave in before his determination. If he needed to hear me speak so at that moment I would do as he desired. What would occur when I returned the next year, if by some wonder or magic he had survived and I found him there, would be another matter.

'Good.' He put a hand to my shoulder, looked at me clear. Though I was pretty much as tall as he already I had the feeling when he stood before me like this that I was looking up to him.

'But, Sir, won't you be needing it, next year won't you have need of it?'

His smile creased no more than the corners of his eyes. 'You forget that I will have the wager.'

THE EXPERIENCE OF
THOMAS CAVE

An uncharted island of Svalbard, the winter of 1616–17

2

IN THE LIGHT of the North distances deceive. The stationary man watches the ship depart, so slowly that the steely band of water before it can barely be perceived to extend. The clarity of the Arctic air is such that even when the ship is far off, sails, masts, details stand out sharp to the eye as if they were still close in, and he has the impression that he could yell out and call back a boat long after all on board are out of earshot. Though he does not will it, a cry of a kind eventually escapes him, a cry that comes as much from the heart as the lungs, and that is swiftly swallowed into the lap and draw of wave on shingle.

At last a single sound comes back to him, a cannon shot that by its faintness confirms just how far the ship has travelled. As if he did not know. He has spent enough time in these seas to recognise such effects of the atmosphere. He has seen an experienced pilot stand to some three or four hours from the shore for fear of running on to rocks that appeared alarmingly close to his eye; then, too, with a slight change in the air, he has seen land appear to recede before an approaching ship, retaining the same clarity and proportion for many hours though the wind would seem to drive towards it, so much so that sailors have become spooked and spoken of being held back by some hidden loadstone beneath the sea. In these regions a man cannot always trust his eyes but must turn to reason and calculation to determine what is before him. And Thomas Cave feels the wind on his cheek, a light breeze coming off the land behind him, cold from the north, and knows that it is taking the ship away though she seems quite still out there in her silence, a fine outline that holds each time he looks back to it, that does not appear to diminish but in the end only to dissolve, all at once, as the luminosity itself disappears from the horizon. He gives a little shake then as if a cloak has been taken off him, looks about him alert as if he has just perceived the cold, the tent behind him, the fact that it is about to be dark. Beyond these simple observations thuds a deeper knowledge which his mind is momentarily unable to process: the enormity of what he has elected to do.

He raises his chin as if to open the passage of his throat so that he can breathe the better, makes a slow inhalation and holds it down until the thought is quelled.

Then he puts his back to the sea and the absence of the ship and begins to walk up the rise of the beach. After a few steps something catches his eye. He bends to take up a stone, a slim grey disc of granite. He weighs it in his hand, sees how fine and perfect it is, how neatly it fits into the curve of the thumb and forefinger as if it were made to lie there, and then he turns again, towards the sea now, puts his side to the waves, curves his back and arcs his arm behind him. With a whip of his wrist he lets the stone fly, on a horizontal trajectory so that it does not strike water until it is many yards out from the wave edge. Once, twice, again and again it skims the dark surface, eight times in all.

Emptiness so resounds about the whale station that it might have been abandoned not for hours but for years. Only the smell, at once cloying and rancid and sooty, and the sheen of grease that holds to every surface testify to its recent use. Even to the man walking back there these structures seem alien: the vats, the cauldrons and boilers, the great low tent of sailcloth that was warehouse and workshop and is now, with a fine string of smoke above it grey before a greying sky, to be his home. Not two decades since this land was known and already man has placed his mark upon it, set down in the wilderness works of a solid, squat ugliness that will never in a hundred years belong. Yet God, he has no doubt, is patient. God will know how small and how feeble are the works of man. How all this will return to ashes and dust. A little way off, spread beside the shoreline, lie the remnants of the carcases of a dozen whales, heaps of bones with a raucous multitude of gulls still picking and screaming amongst them, milling beneath the great white jawbones like the congregation of the damned beneath the arches of a fallen cathedral.

Their racket recedes as he enters his inner chamber, closes behind him the thick wooden door that itself weighs like the door of a church. His hermitage. He kneels before the stove and throws on a slab of blubber that spits and flames up in the half-light. Only that morning there had been a gang of men at work in the room. There was noise, crowding, the stink and warmth of labouring bodies. They had helped him to build the wooden cell inside the walls of the tent, hammering planks, pouring sand. Their absence now is all the more tangible as here in the enclosed space even more than outside their smell remains, an animal reek of bodies and sweat and fish oil, a fetid den smell that he notices only now that they are gone.

The room is barely ten foot square, the stove at the centre of it, the smoke drawn up through an opening in the ceiling funnelled with sailcloth. It is part underground, the floor dug down through the sand to the underlying rock, and the walls above ground are thick, made from two layers of close-fitting deal planks and the cavity between them filled with sand, buckets of the stuff, until a sprinkling of grains welled out between the flaws in the plank seams. It was, he thinks, a satisfactory labour. Insulated in this way the walls will not permit the penetration of the sharpest wind or blizzard however it may swirl about in the tent space beyond; and so muffled it is within the chamber that when he falls still there is only the companionship of the fire to keep him from the sense that he is deaf.

Right up by the stove he has his bed, a wooden bunk laid deep in dried deerskins. The wool of these northern reindeer is thicker than that of the deer of England, the skins more substantial, warm beneath the body and above it as a heavy embrace. They are roughly cured yet do not smell too strong; they will last him out till next summer. The skins and the fire are to be his comforts. Besides these all his furnishings are a plain table and a chair, and the chest, itself overlaid with skins, in which he keeps whatever he has carried about from port to port, a few possessions of use or those that cling to him from the past: clothes, twine, knife, Bible and prayer-book, the cobbling tools with which he once worked on land and which have since whiled away long hours of voyage and waiting, and his fiddle, laid on the top and wrapped about with a length of embroidered cloth.

This he takes out, he unfolds it from the cloth and hangs it on the wall. Not too close to the stove lest it take too much heat. The action of putting out the instrument, laying it across the pegs he has fixed, is a making of home. Gently he handles it, and the fine touch of the wood brings a memory to his fingers. The fiddle has been hung this same way before, once on another wall of wooden planks, beside a square glassless window with a yard and a garden beyond. For a second he caresses it, holds and then with cool self-control dismisses the picture from his mind. In this room there will be no windows, no views of land or sky.

No dreams, he tells himself, but function. This space is designed, fitted, for survival alone. He turns to the things that his shipmates have given him. So much they think a man needs: three muskets, some pounds of shot, a powder-horn and a barrel of powder that he will keep warm and dry before the stove, a sword that he will put beside the door, a prayer-book, an almanac, a telescope, a blank-paged log and a bundle of pens from Captain Duke that he lays neat and square to the right-hand corner of his table. He lays the log down there and hesitates, wonders what record he will make of this day, takes it up again in two worn hands and lays it this time in the centre before the chair. Yet he does not sit, not yet. He goes instead to the door beyond which the provisions were stacked, begins to sort which things he must bring inside the chamber and which can be left out to whatever extreme of climate will occur in the months to come. There are firkins, barrels, casks, sacks; hard bread, ship's biscuits, butter, cheeses, cured meats, dried plums, liquors, sugar, spices. Astonishing to see the complexity of his requirements. They have left him tobacco also, tinder, candles, soap. He begins to lay and sort but has not the heart to finish the job that night. Suddenly he is tired down to his bones, he cannot see the purpose of so many things, so much victualling for him only, just for one man alone; it seems mad and extraordinary luxury as if all a man alone needed might be air.

He will leave everything where it stands, this night at least. He pulls the heavy door to on his cell. In the log he will write one thing only, the title and the date: *The twenty-fourth day of August in the Year of Our Lord 1616. To Captain Thomas Marmaduke of Hull, an account of the experience of the seaman Thomas Cave, his stay at Duke's Cove on the shore of the unexplored territory of East Greenland, the first winter any man is known to spend at that place.*

3

H E SLEEPS HEAVILY that first night and knows no
dream. He wakes innocent of thought in the insulated
room, wakes to utter silence and darkness broken only by
the glow of embers. How long is it since he has slept without
a dozen other bodies snoring, farting, rustling about him? He
closes his eyes again, lies back beneath the weight of deerskins and listens, listens with intensity until he can hear the
distant screech of gulls and a drumming that might be that of
the sea but might be no more than the pulse of blood in his
inner ear. It is an instant more before the knowledge of
identity and place return to him.

Daylight is so very fine and clean that emerging from the
tent he feels as if he has come from some shaft deep
underground. He stands and blinks, his hand upon the
doorpost. The bright paleness of his eyes reflects that of
the sky. Thomas Cave has the look of the North to him even
though he was not born to it: tall, long-boned, gaunt in his
features, fair in his colouring, some austere Nordic gene in

the Suffolk man that gives him ease with this landscape, the spiny peaks, the coldly lapping sea, that gives him also his sureness of movement, walking with loping strides across the scantily covered soil from the tent towards the crease of the rivercourse, along it and away to a slope he knows where the walls of rock curve about and give shelter facing into the sun and the scurvy grass is found.

He carries a sickle and a hessian sack. He has his plan, knows that he must make full use of the daylight and the brief growing season remaining. This day he will cut salad, though salad is a lush name for this grass which is almost the only edible vegetation here, a bitter cress-like herb that the sailors know as a healing plant for ulcers and infections of the mouth, and more importantly as a prophylactic against scurvy. He will work the day through, seek through the bog and across the base of the mountain, fill the sack if enough green stuff can be found and take it in to dry under cover, spread the stalks as once he had done hay on a rack to preserve it through the winter. He knows he is late; stems and foliage are sparse, hard to find, but even the meanest leaves will have value brewed as tea.

Three things they say hold against scurvy: salad and fruit, fresh meat, and activity also, for it is observed among sailors that it is ever the indolent of nature who succumb first to the disease, as if God's judgement might be in it. Only this last point Thomas Cave will not accept, he will not believe such judgements are made on a man in this life but only in the next. His is a modern and reasoning mind, he will not put the cause down to any such superstition but suspects instead that there is some direct correlation to be made there, either that physical activity builds the humours of the body to resistance against the disease or that the lazy have some inbuilt weakness or predisposition upon which the disease may prey. Or it may be that this impression is created only by the apparent indolence of the disease itself, which creeps up on a man and makes him slow and feeble, thins his blood and his fibres so that his lips crack and his teeth loosen, and his energy drains into carelessness until he lies and dies curled on his bunk like a baby with his fists between his folded knees.

Either way he shall hold to his will. If by action he can keep the disease at bay then he shall do so. He ekes his way across the landscape, clump by clump, bending low or sometimes on his knees, looking up at last in surprise to see how the sky has turned colour, how suddenly the sun seems to have slipped down to meet the sea of the bay. It aches to straighten up. He puts downs the sickle and stretches, turns his head in a circular motion to loosen his neck, rubs the muscles of his back where they run down to his waist. His body has become stiff, it is not as supple as it once was. The colour softens and builds, a pink glow that reaches right across the sky and the sea by the time he returns to the tent, the good of the day of labour like a prayer in his heart.

This first day of my sojourn broke clear and fine, for which the Lord be thanked, and I rose early and set about to gather scurvy grass from where I have seen it grow in the lee of the mountain to the south. This I have brought in to the tent and spread for drying there.

No sweetness to its scent as he lays it out but a pungent, sulphurous tang against the smokiness of the atmosphere, the evening air harsh with frost. *When night comes the air is cold, the sky stark and with an icy shimmer to it. I do not expect that I shall find much further opportunity for forage.*

He closes his eyes, yawns, the quill in his hands. What more is he to write? Life is very plain when it is reduced to one day at a time and to that one day's routine of survival. He has worked, returned, begun the arrangement of his stores. On some pages at the back of the log he sets out a list of the quantity of the stores and begins a calculation of the amounts to be consumed each week.

Only three days more the fine weather holds. The last of those days he allots himself for exploration. He has noted how visibility has become startlingly greater than even on the clearest days of summer, when a party of the whalers had gone inland and followed the river course back to the falls and climbed the southern of the two sharp peaks that overlooked the bay. He sets himself the other, northern peak, which is the more rugged, the spinier of the two. So sheer it rises from the beach that he cannot imagine making an ascent from that side, but only from behind, if he is to walk first to the falls and then along the ridge above. He has studied this south-eastern face closely, looking for the possibility of a path, thankful for the angle and sharpness of the morning light which defines and shades each incline, rock and feature of the mountainside as if it were engraved with a fine point.

All is so clear. Distance, foreground, everything has detail. The colours in the stones, the green and yellow blooms of lichen, the stems and reddened leaves of tiny scant plants. The grain of the rock, its cracks and the sharp edges that he can feel even through his boots and that graze the fingers when he must scramble. The mountainside marbled with black ravines, silvery watercourses, snowfields of polished whiteness. The valley falling away beneath him, the blackness of the bog and the glistening of the streams running into it, a tangle of white streaks that weave out and back into one another like the boughs and twigs of a tree.

At the summit there is a wind that stings his eyes to tears. The peak is so sharp that he dare not stand full upon it for more than a second for fear the wind will blow him away. He crouches instead in the lee of a rock, the elation in him holding him taut as a leopard waiting to pounce. Or a watching eagle. Before his eyes an eagle view: throughout his field of vision, mountains in the form of flames, burning white with the sun upon them, and beyond in all directions, smooth and blue-white, a frozen sea.

It is my opinion that this cannot be East Greenland but an island, a place for which we have no name. Our ships had sailed the southern coast and we had thought the land to be a promontory or projection from a greater mainland but yesterday I climbed the mountain to the north and discovered that it was not so, that the place is indeed surrounded by sea in all directions. The sea to the north appears to be frozen so it is yet possible that it may connect by the ice to further land.

On this day, the second of September, I saw for the first time a small quantity of drift ice driving to and fro in the bay, and with the telescope I saw upon one piece far out two sea horses lying asleep. I judged however that they were too far off for hunting.

He saw cloud also, cloud that crept in swiftly from the east as he looked out to sea, that when he turned hung suddenly leaden over the island behind him. The temperature had turned as fast, a sudden drop that was almost as tangible as the loss of light. The first snow to fall since he had begun his time alone was a thin, mean snow, no more than a light fall, just enough to cover the surface of the island, to hide rock and vegetation for one opaque still day until the winds sprang up and stripped some places bare again.

In the snow I have found tracks of deer close to the tent. In the stillness and fog of the previous day I did not like to venture far from the tent for fear that I would be unable to return, but this day it was possible to hunt. I killed a reindeer of good size not one hundred yards from the door. With this in addition to the ship's rations and the birds I have trapped I have hanging in the tent now a good stock of meat.

The deer was a stag and it was clear that it did not know the sight of man. He had worked from downwind, taking every care, walking crouched and with silent footsteps in the snow, and yet just as he came within range the animal had sensed something and looked about and he could have sworn that it looked directly at him, alert for an instant as he had seen deer so many times before, in that intense frozen second before they set to flight. Only this one did not flee but saw him with his arm extended into the musket, taking aim, and put down its great antlered head as if he were nothing animate, nothing more than a piece of driftwood, an alien tree washed up upon the shore, and munched again at some thin mosses where its hooves had churned up a patch of snow.

The stag was too heavy for him to bring and hang inside so he had done his butchery immediately at the site of the killing, with cold hands and the wind swirling odd icy flakes like pinpricks against his face. He skinned, removed the entrails, crudely hacked up the carcase leaving what he did not want for foxes and gulls to scavenge. The pieces he cut off he brought into the tent and there in a copper washed them in vinegar and strewed them with pepper. Suspended between the poles the meat now begins to freeze even as it hangs, leaving on the floor beneath it a pool of iced blood so dark that it is almost black. He has kept back one steak to eat fresh that evening, strong dark meat and very lean.

More deer appear on the following day and he has further success, killing two younger animals, hauling them in to hang in the tent and using pieces of them to bait the snares he has set for foxes. The hours of daylight are short, the sky low, the sun a colour, an idea rather than a form, too often obscured behind a weight of cloud. He feels an urgency to his hunting, each pound of meat to hang and freeze or preserve a piece of time ensured. He does not know what light, what cold, to expect of the winter, nor if there will be any breathing warm-blooded thing to live it through besides himself.

4

*MICHAELMAS. THESE THREE days a blizzard has
kept me in. Its wildness came upon the place suddenly and
with great drama, akin more to an ocean squall than any storm on
land. The cell is sound and snug and resists all but the finest whisper
of a draught though the wind howls within the shuddering walls of
the tent outside and fine snow has penetrated there and piles up in
the corners and on the surfaces of the stores and against the far wall.
Each day once or twice when the fury of the blizzard has by its sound
seemed to drop I have gone to the door of the tent and cleared the
space beyond it lest the snow accumulate so high that I am buried
within.*

There he pauses, and in the vacancy of the moment his
imagination catches the word his pen has formed. Involun-
tarily, he closes his eyes. Every now and then it is so, and the
fear takes him. On his eyelids he can feel the snow falling,
white blotting out the colour, white flakes gathering, bury-
ing him. He can feel the snow in his eyes, growing heavier;
cold on his lips, squeezing between them as between the

seams of the tent; snow, weightless flakes gathering weight; fingers frozen reaching through snow.

No, *buried* he will not say. He will say *cocooned*. He scratches out the first word, spilling a blot of ink, writes the other above, a long comforting word full of encircling 'o's. The snow becomes soft then, a wrapping, a cushion, a downy casing between himself and the outside. In the candlelight, in the silence of the inner chamber, his lips mouth silently what he has written, finding comfort in the forms of words, in the facts stated, the process of stating them, using them to quell the fear.

Lest the quantity of wood be short to last through all the time I may require to spend here, I have made a trial of the fire, setting into the midst of the raked embers a log of elm and piling it over with ashes. I found that it was still alight some sixteen hours after.

That is the sort of thing Captain Duke will want to know. What reason can observe, what the body can do. The Captain has given him the log so that he might record not his thoughts but the facts – the means of survival – so that if he should be no longer alive when the *Heartsease* returns the book will at least testify to the conditions he has met with and the viability of any future attempt to winter in these latitudes.

Two old shallops that lay abandoned on the beach I have broken up and brought in to supplement the store of firewood. I have stored the planks within my cabin, laying them horizontally across the rafters so that they form a rough ceiling and assist in containing the heat of the fire. The labour itself was warming, the wood of the old whaleboats brittle with age and salt and splitting sharply, releasing the smell of ingrained tar, a sharp, smoky smell that itself carried the memory of warmth.

There remains a quantity of driftwood along the bay but I believe this to be a limited stock. Since there are no trees in these latitudes, all the driftwood on these beaches must have come off the coasts of Norway, and since no men have lived here before to have the use of it, I can only guess that what I see here is the accumulation of centuries, of all God's time since the world began, and what I use will take many centuries to replace.

Any thought beyond the practical is an indulgence, a vanity. Vain for himself and for his survival and without interest to any other man. It would be a vanity to think that Captain Duke put a value on his thought, on his person even, for all that he had embraced him at their parting and held him close like a friend.

They had only spoken, spoken properly·man to man, the one time, some few days after the wager was made when the Captain had him called to his cabin and took him into it alone. He had not seen inside of it before and had been surprised at the warmth and homeliness of it, a warm brown furnished room but cramped, where Duke, being only a short man, could stand, but he must stoop to speak with him and yet could not feel at ease to take up the chair that was offered.

The details of the interview have run through his mind many times, so much in it unspoken which he might, just might perhaps, if he had been another man, have found the words for, and in them explanation, meaning, comprehension, an answer to what lay blank inside himself.

'The men have told me of your determination, Thomas

Cave. They say that they would have me hold their money staked against our return next season, yet I will not take it from them until I have your confirmation that you desire it to be so.'

'I do that.'

Only three words there, and those ones came to him clear and without pause. He had said what he had said and did not see cause for the Captain to doubt it.

'You are certain of it? You understand that it is my duty to ensure that your resolution is fixed?'

'I am.'

'You speak it lightly and yet I do not believe that you are a foolish or a foolhardy man. I wonder at your motive. You were riled with Carnock certainly. I know that Carnock is a man can drive a dispute out of any trifle, but I suspect that there is something more to this thing than that.'

He had said that last with his voice rising as if it was a question, but ran on soon as he could see that no answer would be forthcoming. 'Something further between yourself and him? Or something between yourself and God, perhaps?'

And Cave stood with his neck bent and let this question also fall, and the Captain, who was a vivid, energetic, impatient man, ended the pause again before he could respond. He smiled, a vivid smile, white teeth in a dark beard, eyes a strong Celtic blue, and touched his arm and led him out on deck again where the sky was high and he could stand, and turned his head to the bright sea and was speaking again, telling a story just as Cave had begun to form in his head the words that he might have said.

'What you propose to do puts me in mind of something,'

the Captain said. 'A man I met last winter when I was ashore. He was an old sailor who had been out to the Indies early on, fifteen, twenty, years ago. He went with Raleigh on some great voyage in search of Indian gold – a madness of the time it was, every other man in those days when in his cups or in an idle moment dreaming of finding a fortune to top the Spaniards', though never then or now could I begin to believe there's any such thing to be found, no land of gold for me but honest toil and the hunting of whales and a plain trade in oil, bones and blubber and barrels, but then of course I'm a plain man, a straight Hull seaman who works for himself, not a King's man nor a poet. So, as I am telling you, this sailor said they did not hear a whisper of any great mines, saw no more than the tawdry bits of gold the Indians wore around their necks and in their ears, and at the last Raleigh decides to make for home but he wants to take with him to show there the son of some local chief and exchanges for him one of his own sailors whom he leaves behind, whom he leaves in a village of savages on the muddy banks of a great river without any expectation of returning.'

'And what became of the man?'

'My informant did not know. He left the ship when they got back to England and heard no more of the story. But he had not forgotten it. The sailor was hardly a man at all but a boy, barely sixteen years old.'

'His case, Sir, was very different than mine. Firstly, I stay because I choose it for, as you put it, my own motives. And secondly then I know for sure, I am confident that, you will return. You are as you say a man of business not a courtier.'

'Yes, Thomas, I will be back.' And the Captain had him

sign a paper concerning the wager that had been made and showed him the money the crew had staked on it, and locked both the document and the coins into a chest. 'And next year I may bring my own son with me. He also will be sixteen by then. Perhaps it is because of him that I think of that boy.'

'Then I shall meet him.'

'What did you say?'

'Next season, when you come, I shall meet your son.'

And the Captain turned and showed interest in him again. 'You do not have a son, Thomas, no family ashore?'

'Once, sir, I might have had a son. No indeed, in fact, once I did have a son.'

The ink on his pen has dried. The fire in the stove has burned down. No, he will not think that way. Thomas Cave stokes up the fire, watches until the flames burn steady again, returns to the table and cleans and dips the pen.

The changes in the weather here come as sudden and total transformations. At once, a blizzard, swirling, obscuring every single thing, and then as suddenly it abates and there is a stillness and clarity as if all before one's eyes is made from glass. The change of the season however has followed a steady and doom-laden progression despite the tempests and the fluctuations of wind and temperature. Those creatures with whom I have shared the island appeared to understand this. All through the past six and more weeks I have observed the departure of the birds that in the first days of my solitude flocked so densely in the sky along the strand and about the cliffs. Gulls, auks, petrels, guillemots, kittiwakes, others whose names are unknown to me, have grouped and taken off for the south, one species after another until not a screech nor a wing can be heard overhead and the silence begins to deafen. Day by day the appearance of the sun has been limited to a noticeably briefer time until days came when its orb, big, coloured and strangely flattened in form, hovered scarcely a few minutes over the southern horizon though the red glow from it might persist for a long period across a wide band at the foot of the sky. Ice filled all the bay with similar inevitability, appearing first prettily as distant ships with sails, sometimes white, sometimes blue, sometimes tinged pink and lilac as touched by the vanishing light, receding, returning, then becoming permanent as the water about them first steamed and then congealed and froze at last into a hard crust.

It has become my habit to climb each day to a lookout on the mountain behind the beach to catch what best view I can have of the retreating sun — so often that it is possible now in the twilight to pick out the clear path that my feet have trodden in the snow. The last few days the sight of it was so slight that I did not know how much of it existed only in a trick of the eye or the delusion of my imagination, but on this day, the fifteenth of October, not even the finest slip of it did appear. I know that for this year I have now seen the last of the sun. The great cold is coming.

5

THERE WAS A TIME of domesticity before this. A closed room, cold outside, a fire within. When he learned a craft through the long hours of winter afternoons, a trade by which he had thought to earn his living when his life with the sea was done, learned from her father the shaping of lasts, the making of soles and heels, the cutting and stitching and burnishing of leather. Then as now he worked to the sound of the fire in the stove, working against the murmur of steady flames, the crack and fall of logs. Then also life seemed pulled close to the small immediacy of a single square room, a single firelit heart with the world immense and distant outside.

The need for routine has become the more to him as the pattern of the days and nights has disappeared. In September there was an easy sanity to be found in the knowledge that he could depend on sunrise and sunset to mark his hours, then mark the ends of the day with prayer and with a meal. Since the loss of the sun he has attempted assiduously to continue to observe the normal passage of time, setting the rhythms of waking and eating to the times of his prayers, naming the days to himself and marking them down, taking note each day of the length of the period in which some glimmer of daylight still persists in the southern sky, when there is light, say, to read the verses of the Testament or to make out only the titles and heads of the pages, taking when visibility permits an observation of the size and form of the moon and noting it so that he can continue even when that light is gone to keep a precise record of the days of the week and the months as they pass.

He wakes, prays, rakes the embers, resets the fire. In this designated morning, if he does not hunt, he chops wood or makes adjustments and improvements to his quarters, in the simplest contrivances of which he takes a childlike satisfaction. He has extended with a length of sailcloth the chimney hood that overhangs the stove and both improved its draw and reduced the smokiness in the air. Such comforts matter to him greatly. More ingeniously, he has used a sheet of lead taken from one of the coolers to construct a lamp in which he can burn whale oil as luxuriously as the richest merchant in Copenhagen. In this clear glow of light he may sit through the rest of his day, writing his log, reading his Bible, making the wooden heels of shoes.

So many heels he has made already that he has set up a shelf against the wall facing the table and lined them up upon it. So many that one evening he looks up unconsciously from his work and suddenly the sight of all those heels sets him laughing: he laughs at the absurdity of dozens of heels, heels to be paired and fitted to shoes and covered or painted

50

black or red, heels to be worn and danced on and scrape the floor, to sink in mud and clack on cobbles; the ludicrous idea, it seems suddenly to him, of so many people being in existence, even if there were only as many people in the whole of the world as half the number of the heels he has made, two heels each man or woman, the one odd heel on the shelf beyond the even numbers denoting perhaps a one-legged man or someone perhaps like a boy he had known in his childhood whose left leg had ceased to grow after an illness and dangled useless and unshod beside his crutch and the knee of the sturdy right one. He laughs aloud and the sound cracks through the silence of the chamber. He laughs until the tears run at the picture of those frivolous shoes and feet shuffling and hopping about. He snorts and blows air from his nostrils, and when the laugh fades his face is warm and the muscles of it feel unfamiliarly stretched.

And after the laughter his eyes again well over. He looks about him. So many echoes there are in the room as the sound dies. He sees it suddenly with pity for himself, the crude windowless chamber and his attempts to make a home of it, sees how in its arrangement he has in so many details mimicked the other house even when he has not been conscious of doing so. The way he has hung his coat on a hook from the back of the door. The arrangement of his tools laid out as on Hans's bench. The hymnal and the Bible stacked in their place beside the bed. The piece of embroidered cloth with which he had wrapped the fiddle spread and draped like a gull's outstretched wings on the rough wooden wall. The fiddle itself.

He has not played it yet. He has not touched it since he

put it out. He cannot bring himself to play it for fear the sound might set off an avalanche in him. Men said that a sound could do that, though he has never seen the evidence of it with his eyes. Men said that a sound could set snow and ice, a whole mountainside, hurtling down; and here in the North, in the unstable conditions of summer, when the whalers went inland or sailed beside the glacier cliffs they passed beneath hushed and aware. Would music do that also, would music have the same effect on what is frozen inside him, would music set him crashing down?

Yet now for just a moment the silence that has held like a taboo in the room has been broken. He takes the instrument down from its wooden pegs. Not to play it but to handle it only, he tells himself, to run the pads of his fingers down it, to pluck a string and see how far its tune has drifted in the cold. Just one distorted note: a flicker of memory, eyes and a swirl of skirts. He carries the instrument to his cot at the fireside, sits, lays it on his knees, his chapped hands cradling it gently as a baby. In the warm patch of light its wood glows like a conker taken new from its spiny green casing. So much is contained there within its hollow body: the potential of sound and the memory of sound, and not only music but all the people and evenings past, a thousand people, a hundred different places. He closes his eyes, his cheeks still damp beneath them. Slightly, as if a vibration runs through him from the floor, as if the ground beneath juddered, his head begins to rock from side to side. It is not any evening that comes to him but one in particular, a long evening in a northern port that opens with strangers and music and ends with a sense of friends though he could not have put a name to any one of them, with wandering out in the moonlight to find his lodging with the face of a girl in his mind, hot and blue-eyed and washed about with hair.

He went with a Dane from the ship, was taken because the sailor knew that he could play. It was a wedding party though he spoke to neither groom nor bride. He spoke few words of any kind all that evening, only the little smattering of English, Dutch, Danish that he had in common with the rest. Music served him well enough for communication, eye to eye with the other players, nodding heads, fingers, chords, rhythms, ripples of notes; where to come in, to follow, to leave off; patterns mastered and racing to crescendo. Then all about him there were bodies moving, faces turning; grinning mouths, eyes alight, clapping and stamping; and at last the music began to blur and his fingers to slide, and he was aware of nothing so much as one distinct point that stood out to him in the crowd: a mass of hair that fell out of its knot on to a girl's shoulders, dark blonde and so much of it and so thick that it fell in a wave like a mane as she was turned about and cantered through her steps. By this time in the evening the fiddle was a part of him and he played on scarcely conscious of separation between the music and himself, and his eyes followed the flash of the girl's hair as if there was no separation there either, as if it were he himself who was making it spin directly through the action of his fingers, spinning the girl round and out of her partner's hands, spinning her through to the end of the dance. And when the music stopped she sank almost to the floor with a sigh and then after a moment she rose and folded the hair back against the heat of her neck, and for the first time he took note of her face, which was generous and regularly proportioned but would not have been distinctive were it not for the richness of the hair about it and for the wide-open blueness of her eyes.

So brief a time he knew her, that first occasion has not tarnished, still outshines the rest.

There was a shoemaker who had a shop close by the quay. Another sailor recommended him to Cave, saying that this man made boots that were both stout and supple and lasted in the sea and snow. His name was Hans Jakobsen and he wore fine samples of his work on his feet although he could not walk without two sticks, since he had injured his spine in an accident in his youth. When Cave went to find the place he saw the girl again. She was walking on the street that they called the Strand and he asked directions, but she did not tell him that the shoemaker's was the very house from which she had come. Her hair was hidden beneath a linen cap and her neck beneath it was fragile. Her eyes showed no recognition as she spoke to him but that was not surprising since he must have looked so different in the street, just a sailor come to the port and buying boots, not a musician transfigured by his playing; and besides, she had a basket in her hand and her mind was no doubt occupied with what she must buy at market. She accorded him no more than the courtesy she would have given to any honest-looking stranger. Her voice was lower than he would have expected, measured, older, and shared the same quality of calm as her eyes. And that was it, the extent of their first contact. Thank you and good day, and he went in and ordered his boots, and when they were made he came back and collected them without seeing her again, and they were as good boots as he had been told, of thick waterproof cowhide and triple-soled to keep out the cold, so that on the next occasion he came to the port he went back to the shop for more, and saw her again.

On this visit Hans Jakobsen told him to sit and pass the time while he went on with his work before him. The job could be lonely, he said, shut in the shop day after day with only an ignorant boy apprentice and a songbird for company, while all the world came in and went out again. Once in a while he liked a man to stop and report of his voyages and what he had seen. So many years he had worked here by the Strand, since his boyhood, he had learned snippets of many languages and English enough to hear a tale or two. Thomas Cave liked the look of intelligence in the older man, the interest and mobility in his face, the crispness of his movements which showed how fit was his upper body despite the weakness of his unused legs. So he found a seat for himself, which was hard as the shop was small and crowded, with shoes and lasts hanging from the beams and swatches of leather on every available surface, and sat and smoked a pipe in the Dutch style and answered the other man's questions. Rarely had he heard himself talk so much. Jakobsen took a shoe on to his knee for stitching and turned it round and his awl stabbed the leather, so fast and precise that you would have thought all his concentration was for his work save for the sharpness and unceasing curiosity of his questions. How tall were the men he had seen on the African coast? Was it true that their wives had necks as long as swans'? What was this thing they called a banana and how did one taste?

Imagine a fruit yellow and long and curved but thick as the handle of your hammer, he answered, laughing, and the flesh soft as that of a medlar but with the pureness and colour of butter. And through the open door he saw the girl working in the back of the house and he realised by some resemblance in her look and her eyes that she was Jakobsen's daughter. He was glad that she was not married yet.

He passed the whole of the afternoon in the shop and yet he did not get the chance to speak with her. And when he went back up the steps to the street on his two strong legs he felt an envy for the life of the crippled man who went nowhere but stayed in that one place that was his own and had his daughter by him and worked wood and leather in his hands.

These days and nights without form he knows that he cannot afford to indulge his thoughts too much. Given a chance they can become more vital than his reality. The phase of the month without moon is the worst. When there is moon there is light, a light which amongst the snow possesses a wonderful clarity like distilled daylight, and there is also movement, change, the visible passage of time. The moonless days are dead days and those more than any others affect his spirits. On those days more than any others he prays, prays to the Lord that he can resist the temptation to melancholy.

He prays for sleep also, knowing now as he has not known before how sleep may be God's greatest gift: His last creation on the Seventh Day, the culmination of His work. Sleep, it comes to him, is God's order. And in this place where the pattern of time is broken, where the sun is obscured and light and darkness are no longer divided, where the very ocean freezes to the hardness of rock and with the forms of rock within it, it takes an effort of will to hold to God's order. It is a pattern that he imposes upon himself, lying on his cot for the allotted period whether or not his body or, more difficult, his mind, has the inclination to sleep, then rising to observe the rituals of the day. And yet he fears what will in fact be the case: that he will not sleep and wake again in clear and orderly stretches until day and night are re-established in the world outside.

Since that night he let himself think of her, rest has become ever harder. He has only to close his eyes and her image comes to him: a voice, a pair of eyes, a head of hair, that made a city home when for twenty years he had not seen the need of a home. So that he might talk with her he had learned the language, so far as he was able: strange words but clear and plain, so that when he spoke to her he spoke directly and without deviation as if he had been a child.

'What is your name?' he asked. Though he passed the shop often, having made the street an habitual route so long as his ship remained, he had not till this moment come across her again alone.

'Johanne,' she answered. And then, looking up, 'I've seen you talking with my father in his shop.'

'He is good to talk to, your father, I would not have thought a shoemaker would know so many things.'

'Oh, he talks with everyone,' she said, and her affection filled out her voice and made her smile. 'He talks with the people who come to his shop, like yourself. He's always done that. He gets them talking and they sit there like you do and he makes their shoes. Here by the harbour he must have met people from every land in the world by now. He says everyone who comes to him has a story to tell.'

A story. Does he have a story? No, the story is hers, all hers. He is outside of stories. He is just a man alone in the dark, without others to see him and to make him real.

October thirty-first, the Eve of All Souls, and there is a cold glitter in the sky.

Thomas Cave tosses on his cot. The skins are heavy on him but they do not make him warm. He gets out, wrapping the furs about him, and adds wood to the fire, then goes to his table and sits hunched tight, and watches for the flames to rise and for their warmth to touch him.

Johanne kneels to tend the fire and a strand of hair falls across her face. She pushes it back and it is golden in the light of the flames. It is so thick, her hair, he is ever surprised by the weight of it when he takes it in his hand, lifting it back from her neck and shoulders like so many veils, pulling the strands together and holding them in the ring of his thumb and forefinger twined like rope.

Since the sea has been frozen I have seen a number of white bears. Since I have not seen such a quantity before I think it is possible that they have come across the ice, either that or they are hunting farther afield than their usual summer grounds and have been attracted to the fishery by its scent or even — though I fear to think it — by my own presence here. Certainly a number of times I have heard a most menacing snuffling and exploring about the walls of the tent and when the sounds had gone and I dared to go out, I found the snow disturbed and their huge pawprints in it. Once I saw a single bear upwind some two hundred yards off. On account of its white fur, its moon shadow showed almost more clearly than its self, a large bear that held an instant upright like a man and looked about, and then lowered itself and lolloped off, most lightly and easily for a creature of such cumbersome size, across the ice of the bay to where there were many lumps or rocks of ice gathered. I took my musket and followed until I could get within range under the concealment of the blocks of ice. But before I could fire an unfortunate accident befell me. A narrow piece of ice beneath me broke, it was close to where the river flows into the bay and the movement of water must have made the ice in that spot unusually thin, and I fell, my legs at least, into the freezing sea. I threw up my musket, which I was able to retrieve later, and called out, and I can only thank the Lord God that in that moment the bear fled, as I scrambled to find grip in all the rough ice and pull myself up. What was extraordinary was the speed with which the water froze on my boots and breeches, which made them seem dry again before I could begin to shiver.

Since that occurrence I have made a loophole in the door of the tent through which I can spy the bears when they come nosing about. This day for the first time I made use of the hole and by the grace of God it was a success. The bear came so close, so inquisitive it was that I was able to shoot it in the head at close range. Without moving a limb it sank down into the snow. I came out tentatively all the same and finished the job with a lance, thrusting it like a harpoon until the blood oozed velvety black on the moonlit ground. So today I have fresh meat, God be praised, and need not fear the pining of hunger for some weeks yet.

I have cooked and eaten of the animal's liver, of which I had not partaken before, and found it delicious and as I believe full of strength. After I had eaten and said my prayer of thanks I took myself out, and the sky being clear and the air still I took a walk and climbed some way up the mountain where in an earlier month I had gone to look for the sun. This was the longest walk I have taken since that planet disappeared from view. It is noticeable how the sensation of cold varies considerably with the quantity of moisture and of wind in the air, in still dry conditions such as this day causing less discomfort than the cutting sleets of more southerly latitudes. As I walked I beheld an eerie pulsing of lights in the heavens and, on this night of all nights, was moved once more to prayer.

6

A SHIVER RUNS THROUGH him that starts from his guts and yet his head is hot. There is a hammer in his head, beating at his temples. His skin is hot, taut as if it has been burned. He lies half-conscious on the cot, not knowing what is come to him, not knowing even how long it has been so. The fire inside him may have lasted a minute or hours, it is without sense of time. Only the fire in the stove knows time. He watches it burn, flames leaping, subsiding, so mesmerising that when he closes his eyelids they continue to dance through his throbbing brain. And he feels how the delicate skin of his eyelids also is drawn tight, as if it will blister and snap, as if it too has been burned by the fire. He lifts them open again but only to see that this is not so and that in reality the flames have burned right down now and the fire must be replenished. Feebly he gets down from the cot. The shiver runs through him again and his legs are weak as if they were made of paper. Yet before he can work on the fire he must drag himself urgently to the pot beside the door and shit, empty himself as if he is being purged, and then after a long pause when the heat subsides and the cold becomes external and real, drag himself back on folding paper legs, holding first to the table, then the chair, the edge of the cot, barely having the strength to lift a log.

Again he closes his tight-skinned eyes and now drifts into lassitude, into a half-sleep in which the sound of the fire is lulling and the only sensation that remains is a strange tingling that runs over the surface of his body from the soles of his feet to the small of his back, to his neck and ears. His temples feel taut as if fingers were stroking and pulling at the skin, stretching it back to the brain, cool fingers pulling it away, breaking and shedding the first hard layer of skin. His body lies quivering beneath them, naked as that of a snake in its sloughing, passive and defenceless.

He feels her hands on him, her body beside his, her hair falling on to his chest. And he shrinks away. 'Do not touch me,' he says. 'My skin. See, my skin is cracking away. Some illness, some poison in my body attacking it both within and without. My skin cracks and peels away in fine transparent strips. You cannot touch me. My skin cannot stand it.'

She hears him and pulls back, but not so far that he loses knowledge of her presence. She dresses just out of his view behind the high cot, putting on her white blouse, tying the laces at the back of her dress, plaiting her hair into a single long braid that she will twist and fix beneath her cap. Then she will sit and wait for him to recover. She knows how to wait as a wife in port will always wait for a sailor.

'I think that it was the bear meat. Yes it must have been the bear meat, the liver I ate to make me strong. There is some left, over there in the pan. Do not touch it. I will throw it out when I am well.'

How can it be that she is not cold? She has put on a cherry-red jacket but it is only of a thin wool and its sleeves are folded back to the elbow with the white linen cuffs of her blouse folded over them, and her neck rises bare from the loose collar, her skin smooth, soft, glowing with youth. She has left off her shoes and one thinly stockinged foot shows from beneath her skirt. She gives him a demure half-smile and then takes up from her lap the sewing that has somehow come to be lying there, a piece of embroidery with the needle threaded and waiting, turns sidelong to him and begins to stitch, holding the embroidery a little forward of her so that it catches the best of the lamplight.

'When I am well again will you let me show you this place where I live? It is a cold stark place but it is also very beautiful. I have never had the chance before to show you any one of the places where I have been though I have spoken of them to you many times. Virginia where there is tall forest green and unbroken for days' journeying along the coast. The Azores whose islands rise out of the sea like eggshells with villages on white and yellow sands, where the people are brown and swim like fishes and string necklaces of shells that are beautiful as precious stones. London with its river full of masts, Hull, Aldborow where I first set sail and which would not seem unfamiliar to you, though it is a meagre place compared with Copenhagen with but a few fine houses and a wide flat shore, and at its back a long rivermouth with a lip of land to shield it. And of all those places nowhere is more strange than here, and do you know why? It is because here there are no people. None. No one here but our two selves. Yes, when I am well enough again to walk, if the moon be bright – for I do not know what day it is, in my illness I have lost touch with the phase of the moon – if the moon be bright and the weather clear and not too cold I shall take you on a little tour of my beach, my mountains, my hinterland, this little part of the island that I know.

'When I have the strength to move we shall go out, shall we not, look in the sky for the stars which now that it is winter seem sometimes bright as if they are alive, look for God's shimmering in the sky? I shall be strong enough to go out very soon, I think. Though I am feeble the gripes and the shivers have passed, and I shall drink some spirits and a little of this broth here, and will soon be back to my old self though a little raw in the skin perhaps, but that symptom too is receding.'

She puts down her sewing and comes and sits on the deerskins beside him, and her arms are soft and rounded, and her belly bulges slightly where the jacket is unbuttoned, her waist big against the fabric of her dress. She does not touch him on account of the tenderness of his skin but sits quiet beside him until he sleeps.

The lights break serene, billowing bands of green and yellow and carmine red that glow and contract and fade across the great arc of sky above the figure of the man, who is so wasted, purified after his illness that he feels he could be drawn up into them, insubstantial himself as a veil. They glow and transform and quiver, and sudden rays shoot through them, and then as suddenly they vanish and in the moment's pause which, shot as it is with stars, is more silent and more without colour than any moment he has ever known, he sees her upturned face beside him, so rapt in the sky that she has forgotten his presence, her eyes wide, her lips a little apart exhaling a ribbon of condensed breath, her hair fallen from its cap half down her back as she bends her neck. Tentative as if she too might vanish, he reaches out to touch her hair, to pull his fingers through it to loosen it further, to move his hand on and let it rest in the warm hollow of her back. Her two hands have till then been placed soft and flat upon her swollen belly but she moves one now and takes in it the hand that he has free, and without a word pulls it to her belly, beside her own, so that he too through the pads of his fingers and palm can feel the movement of the baby within. The lights flare again, tongues of flame that writhe and lick the heights of the sky, then melt away, and in the moonlight she is no longer there.

That first time he came back from the sea after they were married he had ached for her. He had thought of little but her all the days since they had first sighted land. Yet when they approached the Sound a moist autumnal wind had blown up against them, so that the ship had to tack tediously between one low grey shore and another, laying off a whole day and a night before Elsinore, and he had looked out and imagined her expecting their arrival, waiting even at the quayside with the water black and empty before her. When at last they did come to port, he was one of the first ashore, jumping on to the quay before the boat was tied like a man more her age than his, walking as if he was driven through the crowds of men and women; such a clamour, such a wild explosion of life after six months in the Greenland seas, as if the world had burst into flying shards of figures and costumes, of wheels and cries and animals and heads and eyes and mouths, and he had looked into every young or half-young female face he passed for her face, wondering if he might see it, if she might by some chance have known and come for him, and yet as one woman's features blurred into another's he for a moment panicked and lost the memory of her, and feared that if she were indeed suddenly before him he would not know her.

She was at home. Hans was deep in talk with a customer so he brushed past with the briefest of greetings, down the steps and past the birdcage, into the storeroom with its brown smell of leather, and through into the light of the kitchen. She was there, standing at the table with the light flooding in from the open door behind her. Recognised, there was no trouble about that: no difficulty in knowing her hair, golden where the light caught it, her happy smile, her raised hands that were white with flour, all so familiar; but different too, a woman whose full breasts and curve of belly betrayed her as she came away from the table to greet him, in silhouette before the brightness of the yard beyond the door.

'Don't you know me, Thomas?' She came right up to him

where he had stopped, still within the storeroom entrance, and looked into his face but it did not answer her in the way that she expected.

'Is there something wrong, Thomas? Has something terrible occurred? With the ship, on the voyage? I have been so afraid for you all these months.'

And then he saw the tears that were flooding to her eyes as if they had waited there primed for all of that time. He felt a rush of sorrow then and pulled her to him, touched and smelled her familiar skin, her hair, her flouriness: a sweet clean smell. No, there's nothing wrong my love, all went well, the voyage was a good one and we made much profit. And he crushed her to him and kissed her deep, held tight to him all the life in her, and yet below the kiss lay a strangeness. It was too soon for him, too sudden, this new knowledge of her. There was something mechanical in the action, as if he watched himself embracing his wife, a sailor returning home doing what a sailor does, a sailor kissing the wife who is soon to bear his child, two figures performing as themselves and yet they were not yet themselves but only acting themselves, as their lips broke and joined again, two figures re-enacting Thomas and Johanne.

7

WHERE IS SHE? He wakes in fear and claws for her, thinking that his narrow cot is the wide high bed they had in Copenhagen, and where his hand reaches there is only cold air. A blizzard rages about him, howling with such intensity that he feels that it is right in his ear, that it has entered the vacuum of the cabin, that with mounting pressure it will at any instant blow the place apart and scatter it, man, furs, splinters of wood, flying out across the ice. Oh Lord, let Thou deliver me from the tempest! Oh my girl, where have you gone? He breathes deep and attempts for some moments to control his thoughts. When he opens his eyes again the storm has receded beyond the walls. It seems even to have quietened. The room appears before him again solid and square despite the unsteadiness of the lamplight, which is shaken by the draught that succeeds in penetrating the cracks of the doorway however he may attempt to caulk them.

The blanket he had wrapped about his face is stiff as board

and thickly sugared with hoarfrost where it has soaked up the moisture of his exhaled breath. He understands that he must have been asleep for quite some time and yet all that time he seems to have been constantly aware of the storm. He has heard the scream of the wind, felt its vibration within the cell. He does not need to see in order to picture it: the white flakes invisible in the blackness, whirling in such a terrible, dervish way that you could not tell if they fell from the sky or were driven up from the ground.

I have yet to discover the extremity of the climate in this place. It is no more than December and I must expect that the worst of the winter is still to come, yet I have never before experienced such a storm as the current one, nor such a degree of cold. So suddenly and violently it came, just as I had returned within the tent, that I do not dare to think what might have occurred if it had caught me out of doors. It came without forewarning and without apparent direction, as if it had only exploded in the sky above.

There is a thin coating of ice on the walls of my cabin and on the floor beneath my feet, a frost hanging even on the edges of the chimney hood. So cold it is here that everything that does not face towards the fire is frozen, however close it may be. Even the vinegar is frozen in its cask. The bear meat is hard like rock. I have dragged a great chunk of it right to the side of the fire and cut it with a hatchet until it splits, and it does not begin to melt and bleed until I have it in hot water in the pan and over the fire. I believe that it was the liver alone that poisoned me and in the days since my recovery I have eaten tentatively of the other parts of the animal without ill effect. It would be great shame to waste God's bounty, particularly since there is no knowing when I may be able to venture out again for food.

He melts the vinegar as he melts his water, by taking a hot

iron from the fire and placing it into the cask. It cracks and steams like a sorcerer's cauldron and the acidic smell rises into the room. His beer also is frozen though the barrel is only a few feet from the stove. He is disappointed that when it has been thawed what pours off it is no more than sour and yeasty-tasting water, as if it has lost its essence in the cold. But that is so with everything here, every real thing seems numb and without essence. Survival itself is a numb activity. He eats without appetite. He performs routine tasks listlessly as if he has lost the sense of their purpose. He writes his log, and when he dusts off the words and reads them back he does so without emotion, seeing only that they are well formed on the page.

The storm has lasted now some days without change. The ceaseless howl of the wind and the knowledge of the blackness weigh most heavily on my spirit. I endeavour to occupy myself and as I await the Lord's compassion I have repaired my clothes and made the heels for fifty pairs of shoes. Two or three times a day I cast myself down in prayer. I pray to the Lord that He may hold me sane as well as alive until I shall see His blessed sun again, that He will hold me to this Earth, for there are moments when delusions and dreams come to me more vividly than my actuality.

He writes this and knows that what he writes is not the full truth. But is a man's diary ever the truth? Isn't it always an invention, an idea of a possible truth which he uses to control his understanding of himself? He dips his pen again into the ink that he keeps warm by the edge of the stove.

The truth is that the hardest thing to bear through these frozen days has not been the dreams but the absence of them. The loneliness. He remembers how it was in his illness, how she came to him and slept by him and was a comfort to him. She has not come to him again since the storm began, since that moment when she stood out there beside him beneath the sky.

A short time before the onset of this storm I beheld a most amazing display of lights in the heavens. They appeared high above the north-west horizon and played until the very zenith of the sky was lit with shooting rays of fiery colours such as I had not seen before. No sooner had these vanished and I myself returned and closed myself within the fastness of the tent than there came a rush of sound and the wind began its awful howling. As I had seen no other indication I begin now to wonder whether this very phenomenon of the lights may not have been a harbinger of the weather that was to come.

He writes at the table with the light beside him, puts his pen once more to the ink and sees in the corner of his eye the movement of a shadow against the wall. He looks up, but there is nothing there. The effect can only have been due to the movement of his own arm across the light. He reaches again, experimentally repeating his previous action, and there it is, the same dim shudder. He feels a touch light on his head, but it is no more than a flake of ash that has detached from the chimney. He puts a hand to his eyes for a moment's rest, but pulls it away and opens them sharply, thinking that he has heard the rustle of her skirt in the sound of the flames.

He opens his door at last, clambers up over driven snow. Every surface reflects the moonlight, white and smoothed as the wind has left it, the form of the tent gone into a dune, the boilers, the two remaining shallops, every mark of the whalers erased, his footprints gone from the ground. There was a path he had made to a pool far along the beach where water still ran from beneath the glacier and since the beginning of winter he had been able to break through the ice. It is quite lost now, the landmarks about it eerily altered. He sees that he will not find the spot again but must melt snow for his drinking until the ice itself begins to thaw. He brings out a half-barrel and fills it, ramming his shovel against the hard crust.

The aurora that appears as he works comes without colour or pulsation. He perceives only an increase in the light about him and looks up to see white shining clouds in the sky. Like high cumulus, he thinks, soft and woolly like lambs, but they come and go without pattern, without wind to drive them. And before he turns his eyes back to the ground he sees that she is standing not twenty yards off where the beach merges with the ice.

The air is cold enough to pain his nostrils and freeze a rime on his beard and yet she has only a shawl wrapped about her jacket and her hands tucked into it as into a muff.

'With the baby,' she says, 'I am always warm. It is like a stove within me.' And she is big like a stove and he puts his hand to her so that it might warm him too.

And then she walks off ahead of him and he follows, leaving a single line of new footprints in the untouched surface of the snow. As the aurora dims she becomes no more than a shadow, wavering and faintly drawn. So the Lord led His People through the Wilderness, a cloud by day.

On he walks in a state of strange elation, out over the frozen sea, past rocks whose outline he might know and others that he does not know. Ahead she goes, becoming fainter before him until at last the aurora is gone, as if it had never been there, and she is gone with it. Quite gone, not a sign, not a track of her remaining, so that he must know the truth that he has held ignored within him all the time: that she was never there. She was a delusion, his warm and lovely apparition. And if that, then who had brought her to him? Could it be that it was God, bringing solace to him in the darkness, or was it some other? He wakes, it is like a waking, and sees where he has come to. So far. A little time more, another step and another, a dimming of the moon-light, and she might have led him to his death, drawing him, enticing him so far out on to the ice on this night of all nights, this stark night when the snow has fallen deep and orientation is lost. And he had likened her in his mind to the Lord who led the Israelites in the desert. What pride, what blasphemy! He feels the breath chill before his lips and questions if he deserves to live. Yet God is merciful and the moon stays with him. Looking down, he can see his footprints in the snow, and they are indented just enough and the light is just enough for him to make his tentative and shamed way home.

He bends first one and then the other stiffened knee onto the wooden floor, puts together his frozen hands and prays, begs forgiveness for his temptation. She is no work of the Lord, he knows that now; she is not to be confused with any sign of Him. She is weakness and superstition, the softness of his mind. He sobs out contrition along with thanksgiving and vows that he will be seduced by her no more.

His flesh feels sore as if he has been beaten by the cold. One of the fingers of his right hand is blistered by the frost. He rubs it with alcohol, wraps it, and writes with great awkwardness in his log. He chooses not to record his misadventure: *December twentieth, by my reckoning, a Friday. I shall keep this day following the cessation of the great storm as a day of fast in gratitude for my deliverance.*

No recognition, but only the memory of her will he keep. There cannot be sin, he tells himself, in memory.

As that winter hardened the baby grew within her. She seemed healthy as a cow, he thought, and he saw her fatten all over, saw her cheeks become round and red as apples and began to laugh to see the size of her coming through the narrow cottage door.

As she approached her time her back began to ache and her ankles to swell and she was awake often changing her position in the night. 'I cannot lie comfortably,' she said, 'he is pressing against me.' He, she was sure that it was he, on account of his apparent length within her and the size she was with him. And she would take a pillow and arrange it beneath a part of her and for some time the new position would allow her to rest. Thomas Cave however lay wakeful those nights watching her shadowy outline and listening to the steadiness of her breath. He knew that soon enough she would wake again and that in the darkest hour of the watch there would be fear. The child would turn within her and she would wake again clutching her belly as if he were already breaking out of it.

'He is too big for me, Thomas. I dreamt that he had the long bones of a whale. I saw the bones that came from Greenland, long curved bones that you said came from the jaw of the beast.'

'Nonsense,' he said, and moved on to his side behind her so that he wrapped her in his length. 'You must not let such thoughts prey upon you. You who are so young and fit. It is only that you do not have a mother to tell you so.' He put his arm about her and stroked her calm again, and yet her fear had communicated itself to him as he silently recalled that her own mother had not lived beyond her birth.

There was a woman in the district who knew about these things. He did not feel at ease with her. She had a thin white face and long teeth, and her hair was all put away in a cap as if she might be bald beneath, and yet her ugliness did not prevent her from talking good sense. 'No whale my dear but too much cheese you ate. Those bones you feel will be the boy's legs, for with that shape you have he'll be a boy for sure, and a tall one. Have you not seen how they are, a newborn's legs? They come out bent from being so long cramped up inside, bent like those of a trussed chicken.'

Yet she gave her an ale that she had brewed from sage and other herbs, and returned on the following day and felt Johanne's belly again, and this time she rubbed both her belly and her back with oils of violets and poppies. He saw then that she had soft white hands like those of a lady and that her fingernails were trim and clean. He had more confidence in her, seeing that, and chose to walk with her back to her house. A ship had just come in at the quay and the street was packed with its comings and goings. Their talk was interrupted often as some hasty figure divided them or they must step aside before a trolley or a cart.

'She's all right, isn't she?'

'She's young.'

'And strong. You've seen her.'

'She looks strong enough.'

Again he tried for reassurance.

'The fear is all in her mind, don't you think? You must see that often, the first time.'

'See that she drinks that ale I gave her each morning when she wakes. That will make her strong and help her to hold the baby until her time.'

'And the baby, the baby's well?'

A sailor brushed between them and when they came together again he had just a glance from her small brown eyes. 'Keep some pears in her chamber. Good, big pears. That will stop it from coming too soon.'

That was the week of Christmas. They spent it warmly, the three of them, Johanne, her father and himself. He had money still from his Greenland voyage, and he went about the city and bought them gifts, a length of fine russet wool for Johanne and a piece of fine-tooled Cordovan leather for Hans. He felt sure now that he would be able to settle with them on land, was impatient even to do so after so many years. Just once more would he go to sea, in the summer that followed, and with good whaling bring back enough to set them up. Johanne cooked a goose and for those days she too was happy and seemed to lay her fears aside. He took his fiddle down from the wall and played to them, and if she could not dance in such a lively way as she had before, then she could get up in her pleasure and stamp her foot or clap her hands and sway from side to side so that her loosened hair flowed behind her. Without a word Hans took up his sticks and hobbled away to bed, and he played on and was proud of her, so grand in scale that she might be a figurehead and break the waves and lead men out to sea.

Christmas Day. In celebration I have cooked the last of my hung store of venison stewed with plums. I have awarded myself a flagon of wine and seven inches of tobacco. It has been a mild day, for which God be praised, and I have forsaken my habitual chores and eaten generously and sat long at my table like a lord. At noon I left the cooking upon the stove and took a stroll outside. For a brief time I saw a faint white glow on the horizon that tells me that the glorious sun shines on the day far to the south. I take comfort from knowing that December nears its close and the deepest of this long night is passed.

Strong, heavy food it was, a hunter's food, the meat a little high but the plums and spices and the long cooking made it tolerable enough. Sometimes his gut pines if not with hunger then with need of some other thing to eat. The grasses he gathered lasted well but he has nothing left of them now but a handful of dry and brittle strands. All that he has is dried, salted, preserved, rancid. It is almost a pain to him to imagine greenness, the first bite of an apple, or to think of the freshness of milk, butter, new cheeses, white foods soft as women.

Johanne drank much milk. She had a child's milky breath, a fringe of white about her upper lip. And he brought her sweetmeats as if she were a child, exotic foods, cakes cooked with cinnamon. Any delicacy she wanted, he would go out into the city and find it for her. He allowed himself a little money for luxuries from what he had put by.

'These I got from a sailor from Portugal, candied plums. They are said to be the finest in all of Europe.'

The fruit was the size of a bantam's egg, green like an artificial jewel and glistening with sugar. She ate it delicately, savouring its strangeness. 'You must not do this, Thomas Cave. Not only will you make me fat but you will spoil me for a lady.'

But giving it to her was like giving a sweet thing to a child. He could not resist the way she glowed at a treat. Her eyes lit up and her cheeks became all the pinker, so touchingly young and round beneath her little cap.

That January ice stretched right out across the Sound and the city authorities paid gangs of vagrant men to cut a channel more than a sea mile in length, from the edge of the ice all the way into the town. Down this came a brave Dutch vessel laden with other precious goods from Spain, fancy metalwork and tooled leathers as well as foods and wines. This ship became the centre of a great market on the ice to which all kinds of pedlars came, and also the farmers of the district bringing their produce in carts and sleighs. He thought it a fine and memorable sight, the festive crowd spilling out from the quay on to the frozen sea, lone figures of skaters in the flat white distance, the tall buildings of the town behind, the static ship at the heart of the crowd, sails furled, masts bare, tall like a building itself above the ice.

'Come out this once, Johanne, it'll do you good.'

In two weeks she had barely left the house. She said that her head ached and that she felt a throbbing in her, and her legs hurt when she stood, for all that the old woman had pressed and soothed with her fingers and fed her ales and potions. 'No, I shan't come with you,' she said, 'not into such a crowd. But you go, go and then tell me all about it after.'

'Then what shall I bring you?'

'How can I say until I know what there is?'

'Just give me a hint, my love, of what you would most like. The ship's come from Spain, you know. A land of sun and gold, the richest country in the world.'

Johanne laughed at his eagerness and looked about her at the simple room, the whitewashed walls, the wooden floor, the square glassless window with the shutter half across it and the grey chill of winter outside.

'Bring me a piece of its sun then!'

So he went out alone and saw the spectacle. The ice was frozen right across to Sweden and from there came sledges pulled by tough shaggy ponies that looked far too small for the weight behind them, for the drivers who were huge men in wolfskins and for their loads of furs and meat and wood; and other sledges driven by men and women in coloured and fur-trimmed felts who sold hunting knives and fish hooks carved out of bone. There were braziers where men stood and warmed themselves from the inside with fiery

shots of liquor, and he stopped at one of these and went on
with sparkling eyes and bought himself bread and charred
meat to satisfy the sudden sharp hunger that came upon him.

Close beneath the ship he found a crowd gathered about
three of the Spanish sailors who played pipes and drums, and
in the space before them was a tiny creature dancing. At first
he thought it must be a very small child, but fine and nimble
and not sturdy like the toddlers he was used to knowing, a
delicate child in a green silk dress weaving gloved hands in
the air and hopping from one little fur boot to the other.
Then the creature turned its head to the sound of the drum
and he saw that the look on its face was weirdly still, its blue
eyes, despite the sinuous movement of its body, fixed and
quite unblinking. For a second he looked and did not
understand, and then at some apparent signal from the pipe,
the creature set its little hands to its neck as if to lift away its
head. One, two, a roll of drums, and the blue-eyed baby face
came off, and beneath it was another one, the wizened,
brown, wide-grinning face of a monkey: the dainty dancer
was no child at all but a monkey, wearing the head of a life-
sized doll. He was so disturbed by the sight that he was
suddenly glad that Johanne had not come and seen it. At
another sound from the pipe the monkey made a bow, to
the right, to the left, to the crowd before it, and took up a
red-lined box to collect its pay. Thomas Cave held out a
coin and when it came close he thought that its grin seemed
a grimace and saw how its arm shivered and its teeth were
chattering, and he felt pity that it had its nature taken from it
and that it was so far removed from home and climate. What
were men to take a free creature so and play with it and make

it like a human? When he went on he was sobered so that the cold began to get to him and drive him in.

For Johanne all he bought was an orange. It was one that he chose with care from a tall pile, and big enough to fill his hand.

He brought it home and gave it to her, and for three days she treasured her piece of sun on the stone window-sill until she could resist no longer. She took it down then and peeled the skin with clumsy fingers and broke it open, and the tang of its scent shot through the room.

8

AGAIN SHE IS there about him. During this spell of
hard still days he has relaxed his vigilance and let
himself think about her, and his thoughts have brought
her back. Even if he does not see her he knows her presence,
the slow rustle of her movement about him, her soft breath.
'Oh Johanne, who would have thought it could be like this?
The cold is not at all as I could have imagined. The sensation
of it when I step outside, how it strikes deep in the stomach,
how my muscles seem sore from the effect of it as from a
beating, the way it burns as if God made my nerves and
sinews to react to fire but never to know this degree of cold.
Even here inside the cabin I have touched a piece of metal so
cold that it burns and clings to the fingers like birdlime and I
must warm it or tear my skin before it can be released. Once
too hastily I put a stoneware mug to my lips to drink and it
stuck to my beard and lips. It is more intense than anything I
could have anticipated but at the same time more bearable. It
astonishes me how the time passes and the fire burns down

and is built up again and I shape my day between sleep and work and meals and prayer and continue to endure. I eat little, sleep much. I become like an animal that hides itself through the winter and sleeps until spring.'

Beneath the weight of his rugs, he knows her. He knows the hardness of her pregnant belly. That had surprised him at first, its hardness. Her belly is taut like clenched muscle; it has not the softness of woman to it. And because of it he must take her differently and she must come on him. Slow she comes on him, taut, hard, strong, like a ship climbing a wave. Her face is strange and her eyes are closed and her breasts full as sails, the veins showing in them, the nipples dark and roughened and distended, and he closes his eyes also and has no thoughts in the surf.

After, there are words again, easy words.

'Do you remember last winter, Johanne, how cold we thought it? How we said to each other that it was one of the coldest we had known? Day after day of biting north-easterlies and the sky leaden and damp above us. On the streets within the town, ice froze layer upon layer so that walking out was like walking on uneven bubbled glass, and horses slithered and people fell and broke their limbs. It became worse as the weeks passed, with every further melt or snow fall or new freezing, and down every alley the tipped water from household pots made hazards or thin-iced traps. You of course stayed inside most of that time. You wore that red jacket that you loved, with only the top buttons fastened now as you were so big, and a dark shawl over it sometimes and a heavy dark woollen skirt. You sat in a pool of warmth with your swollen ankles up upon a stool and stitched or made tidy pieces of lace. I remember that I thought your stillness very beautiful, the huge wrapped calm of you. Even so there were times when you shivered and looked pinched and you complained of chilblains in your fingers that made it hard to handle the little wooden bobbins.'

He speaks to her in his mind, not breaking the silence. He would not dare to, as if he knows that the brashness of his voice would drive her out. He is aware of her unreality even as the words rise within him.

'I think that I had never lived in such a way before. Not since I was a child in a home I never told you of, in a village two days' walk from the sea, and when I was young I did not see it thus. I was impatient then to be away and my father sent me at the age of twelve to learn the sea from a cousin, his mother's sister's son, in the major port along that stretch of coast. It was where in a sense my life, my life as myself, my life as I could tell the story of it, began. Not in the village, not as the small child I was. I have little memory of him, only a picture of a sober boy who had a mother who was gentle and carried about with her ever smaller children than himself, until one day she died and was not there, and left him with his father and five brothers. I do not think I could tell you more about that early time.'

He is surprised at himself. He begins to be carried away on his words. In this solitude he has begun to look within himself and into his past in a way that he has never done before. He has always been a silent, contained man, but not a thinker. He has lived a life of action surrounded by other men and he has vested his interest in material things. That has been his philosophy: to act, to work, to understand the mechanics of what he does. Not to indulge in pictures and dreams and chameleon memories. Now he feels almost a guilt at what she has tempted him to do, as if it is a sin.

He opens his eyes. He has had them closed to let the pictures run through his head. He wills himself to rise. As though if he did, if he acted like a man beginning an ordinary day, the sun itself would rise, the world melt and come to life outside, the stream run again across the beach, the sea begin to swell and move. But for now his will lies frozen. He seems to have the strength only to turn on to his back and look up to the rough wooden ceiling. He feels his stillness on him like a weight, like the furs holding him down. Something in the fire hisses and draws his attention, and though he does not look he pictures her there seated beside it, seated upright in the chair gently making lace. It has not occurred to him before but perhaps, now he thinks of it, she is a little like his mother.

'It was so very different, that winter when I was with you and the Sound froze over. The type of cold so very different my love from here. Here cold is wholly another sensation.'

His thoughts turn, repeat. What is he doing, talking to someone who is not there? He is tired. He huddles in the furs on his cot. It is not the cold that he fears most now but the inertia of his existence. It may be that the inertia itself is a product of the cold and the incessant dark and of his poor rations, but it is that which he feels crushing his soul: inactivity, enervation, indolence. He lives in constant fatigue, he drifts between waking and sleeping, his brain turning without focus, his identity becoming frozen, clear and yet thick, opaque as ice. Speaking to Johanne reminds him who he is. Was. Again he sees her, gazing vacantly now at the fire with the circle of lace forgotten on her round belly.

'Did I tell you, Johanne, of the time I went to the Americas? We sailed across the mouth of a great river so wide that it was like a sea, and on its shores was a jungle so dense that a man could not step into it. Captain Duke when I was talking with him here – just the other day it seems, though it was in truth many months ago now but they have passed without time – Captain Duke spoke of this very same river and made mention of a boy who was left there by Raleigh, not there where my ship went but far inland along its banks. I think of him in these days because of some similarity and at the same time contrariness in our situation. I wonder if the ship went back, if he survived to see it, if anyone ever found out what became of him.'

It is such a small thing, one boy's fate beside the great brown river and the hugeness of the jungle. He has tried to imagine the boy walking alone in the heavy green heat. He pictures an impossible tangle of vegetation, a rich and rotten smell, a seething abundance of life, but he cannot see the boy there. The boy is insubstantial to him, a wisp, a wavering mirage before the substantiality of the place.

Just then he hears a great crack like a gunshot reverberating across the island. It is the sound of the ice cracking: whenever the temperature dips sharply the place resounds with the writhe of the ice.

And who is he, Thomas Cave? A man from Suffolk strayed into the empty enormity of the North. A man of experience, unlike that boy, with a life behind him. A grown man without love or issue. A wintry stalk of a man, dried-up and hollow inside. A man who makes the wooden heels of shoes, who used to be a sailor, who once played the violin. A man who lets a ghost draw his thoughts, and speaks to her as if she is real as himself.

He cries out suddenly in fear. 'Johanne, why do you come to me? Did you come with the lights? I have heard men say that there are souls in the lights, the souls of the unborn but perhaps those of the dead also. Or do you come from my mind? Is it that I am so astonished with the snow?'

Is this the beginning of it, then? Is this how a man falls prey to what is in his mind, how the madness and the scurvy will get to him? But Thomas Cave has always been a resourceful man, rational and pragmatic. He will not give way so easily.

A man is what he does, God is his witness to his actions. A man who does nothing is nothing. So he will go out. He will hunt. He will not let her take him.

There are sealskins in the outer cabin, scraped and dried, frozen in a pile stiff as planks. He breaks one off and brings it in, and when he has melted and softened it he cuts it to make a mask. He fits it around his head, cuts slits for his eyes and a round hole for his mouth, ties it with cord. He wraps his neck and head in a woollen shawl and puts on his hat and great coat of wolfskin over all, fits his hands into fingerless woollen gloves with clumsy skin mittens above. When he steps outside he is scarcely human in appearance, a slow cumbersome beast with a musket on his shoulder.

For three successive nights there has been a great white ring about the orb of the moon. The light is so bright that he casts a neanderthal shadow on the snow. He seeks other moving forms in the stillness. For minutes at a time he watches an upstanding rock to see if it will move, or a cask left on the beach and blanketed in snow that may at a distance be a lurking bear. He examines shadows, scours the white ground for the patterns of prints. He believes that there are bears about. In the last few days he thinks he has heard them snuffling about the walls of the cabin though he has not caught sight of one. But either he imagined them or the wind must have swept away their tracks and there are now only the marks made by his own feet in their broad snowboots, meandering out towards the mountain and then back along the ice. He does not return until his fingertips begin to burn with the frost inside their gloves. His stomach feels bruised but he does not know if it is with the cold or with the longing for fresh meat.

9

SOME DAYS THE cold is so sharp even within his chamber that he must warm stones at the fire and wrap them and hold them to the small of his back to keep himself from freezing. He huddles curled, immobile, within the few square yards of warmed space before the stove, his awareness so dulled that he cannot reckon the hours.

And yet he preserves his discipline.

Whenever the temperature rises, just so much as to lift the numbness or the pain, he forces himself out. He takes up his skins and a musket, and hunts. Even were there no chance of prey the affirmation implied in this activity would help to keep him alive. As it is, if there is prey to be had then he will find it.

His shipmates have always known him for his skill at hunting. It was a knowledge he brought with him out of his boyhood on the land, a knowledge of tracking and trapping that he had learnt before ever he saw the sea. He is proud of his skill and has always been among the first to go ashore for

meat in whatever place he has come to, be it these Greenland shores or the hot coasts of Africa or the Americas. He
has shot antelope and alligators, he has caught green para-
keets on limed twigs, set snares for monkeys and lizards,
brought down such other nameless extraordinary beasts that
he thought would amaze the people of his distant home.
And yet it is all one, whether you trap a rabbit or an
armadillo. It comes down to a question of instinct: the
eye for the pattern of an animal's movement, the tension
on the thread of a snare. Instinct, and patience.

By the end of January there is a twilight lasting hours on
end. He watches through it, watches for movements of
shadows, for indications of life, and the minutes pass and his
mind seems to fall between them into other times. There
have been so many waitings in his life: the waiting in port,
the waiting on ship, waiting through calms, waiting for
wind, waiting for the child. He looks out into the long
twilight and it seems to him that he has been waiting all of his
life. There was a waiting in the English winter when he
would go out with his slingshot to hunt the pigeons that
roosted in the trees on the commons before the river, he
going out early with his brother into the mist and watching
through that long vulnerable moment before dawn. So
many years it must be since he has thought of that. A
half-light like this, and yet it was not like this, for there
he knew that it would soon be over, and the birds begin to
call and colours break the sky. Here in the North there is no
relief: the hung moment extends to the edge of his endurance. He wraps himself tighter against the cold, plods further
into the snow, searches, checks traps, moves on. Sometimes

he tracks a bear a long way and must turn back daunted at the distance it would appear that the animal can cover, the speed with which it seems to travel. And yet always he is back before the twilight dims, and it lingers longer and longer so that it begins to seem a ghostly kind of day.

Whenever there is a chance of it I take out the musket and look for game. I have had no success since that great bear before Christmas, more than one month past, though I have made a number of sightings. My situation is not yet desperate though God grant that I may have an outcome soon.

It being close to the end of January and thus by my calculation a halfway point in my stay here I have these past few days made a thorough inventory of the stores remaining to me and their condition. I still have a fair quantity of dry stores, biscuit, sugar, cheese. All the ale and wine has frozen in its casks yet the wine at least is palatable when thawed. I am confident that if meat be forthcoming I shall have stores sufficient to last until the summer. Even so I have designated Wednesday a second day of fast in the week, in which I shall subsist on water and biscuit alone, in addition to the Fridays I have kept until now.

He continues to be meticulous in his reporting of the material things of his existence. He does so because, he tells himself, that is what interests Marmaduke – daylight practicalities, the physical things of life – but also, and this he knows but will not put into words, because the writing of this log holds him steady, every detail he writes, each bag of sugar that he counts, like ballast on his imagination. On the pages at the back of the log he has listed his inventoried stores and ruled lines down before them so that he can record in columns neat as those of any accounting housekeeper the quantities consumed. It has become a part of the preparation of each little meal he has: the measuring and the making of an entry in his little book; another piece of his monastic rule, like the saying of his prayers, the reading of his Bible, the making of another pair of wooden heels.

'You are a methodical man, Thomas, I never knew a man so methodical as you.' Johanne had watched him as he brought in his things for the first time, unpacked them into the room above the shop that was to be their own. He put his Bible on the table before the window, folded his clothes into the chest at the foot of the bed, set pegs into the wall from which to hang his fiddle. He was conscious of the way she looked at him, with a kind of tender respect that made him feel wiser than he was.

'It is so many years at sea,' he said, 'carrying about with you just a few things that you can call your own. It makes you tidy with them.'

It was not such a remarkable thing to say but she received it as if it was. Perhaps that was part of why he liked so much to be with her, that she gave him identity. She laughed at his jokes, took his thoughts as wisdom, touched him and made his body more alive.

Her breath is a warm draught down his neck.

'Such a methodical man, Thomas Cave.'

He hunches over his log, a monk-scribe resisting temptation. Only a crack in his thought and he has let her in.

*I was disturbed this morning to discover when I went to fill my
powder-horn that one of the powder-bags I had in store had somehow
become damp and frozen. I have brought the bag as close to the fire as
I dare to lay it and spread its contents to dry.*

'I wish my dear that you would not read over my
shoulder.'

'But Thomas you know that I cannot read.'

'In that case will you not see how by standing there you
press in on me and take the light?'

He does not turn to see her but looks fixedly ahead, his
tight words spoken from tight lips. Always he has been a man
to hold his feelings tight. This is not Johanne, he tells himself,
this is a phantom; he might rage at her if he would and he
need feel no guilt. If only she would go. He wants her quite
gone, out of his light and out of his mind. He pushes the
chair back and it grates like the anger held in him. For the
second time in a day he puts on his furs, takes the musket, the
horn, the shot, and goes out into the cold twilight. He will
not look back though he can sense her there watching. Such
a glow there is in the sky now, such hints of dawn colour,
that he can scarcely believe that the sun will not appear
within minutes above the horizon yet he knows that it will
not. For days this light has tantalised him and put his nerves
on edge.

He decides that he will climb the mountain behind the
beach where he last saw the sun. Each day conditions permit
he will do that now, climb the mountain or at least to the
lookout and watch for the first moment that the sun returns.

95

It was always a steep climb and it is the harder now, as his old path is all gone and he must remember his way and tread it out again. Close to the summit he pauses, panting for breath, and looks down the way he has come. The slope looks smooth in the flatness of the light, steep and perfect as a sugar cone, a lilac glimmer to its surface. It looks as if he could sit and give a great push with his arms and slide back down on his behind smoothly as a child at play, slither right down to its base and come to a slow halt on the beach below. He follows the gradient with his eye, back down the way he came, and starts suddenly to see movement down there on the path he has made. Just movement he sees, for in the twilight he cannot make out the form, which is no more than a smudge on the snow.

He climbs on, turns again. The pale shape follows his path, but closer now. All he need do is load the musket and wait for it to come within range. So lightly it moves, slowly gathering form as it approaches, advancing uphill with easy light steps, tracking him. A big bear, it seems, though he knows from experience how thick the fur is on these Greenland bears, how much bigger they look than they are when it comes down to meat and bone. He holds his breath as it comes, the wind blowing fine grains of snow into his face, wondering if at some point the bear will decide that his tracks are too fresh, will become wary and begin to circle round. Lord, let it not be so. Let the beast come close . . . The bear pauses, stands a moment on its hind legs, disconcertingly like a man, and sniffs the air. Thomas Cave fires the musket, directly at its head. And the animal lets out a great howl and is thrown backwards down the steep mountainside, somersaulting over again and again and continuing to howl as it falls. The sound stuns him where he stands above it in the landscape. It is so long since any sound of life has been heard here, any sound so gruesomely redolent of flesh and blood. Over and over it rolls and at last comes to rest against a rock.

He follows cautiously, reloads the gun, fires again at close range. The howls fade to whimpers and, at the last, a wet gurgle in the creature's throat. He goes and stands above it, like a bear himself in his furs. Deep inside he is hot, exalted with the killing. A grand beast bigger than himself, meat to last him many weeks, if he can get it home. See, woman, what a man can do. Out here, even here, where one man is so small, so minute on the face of God's frozen Earth.

10

'FATHER SAYS THAT you do not need to take ship again when the child is born. He will have you work with him in his shop. He says that you have good hands.'

'The sea is what I do. I shall go, for the season, but I shall return.'

'Last year when your ship did not come, I was afraid for you. Will you not stay with us?'

'There's money in a whaling voyage more than your father could dream of in a lifetime. I shall go back, once, twice, until we have what we need. But do not worry, I shall come back to you. Perhaps, if there have been many whales and a good season, we can build ourselves a new house, a bigger house than this one, somewhere new but close so that Hans can move his shop but people will know it still.'

'I should like that. But I should like to stay somewhere near to the Strand.'

'Or we could move to the island. They are building many

new houses there. I saw when I went walking there just the other day.'

'A house with a carving about the doorway.'

'Perfect glass in all the windows.'

'With furniture made of oak and pictures on the walls.'

'A tiled floor, black and white in chequers.'

'And a rug on it to warm our feet, placed just so.'

'And you shall have a fine new dress, or dresses, many dresses, and white aprons, and collars of the most delicate white lace.'

'And caps, please, and ribbons, and silk threads for my embroidery!'

'And oranges to eat whenever you please.'

'I shall dry some of them then and put them out to scent our rooms.'

'And our children shall run in and out through the open door and see the ships and tell us who has come and from where and what they have brought with them.'

'How many children shall we have?'

'Oh, very many. After this one, many more.'

And Johanne fell silent and looked into the fire and he saw how her hand stroked her belly and did not know if she was conscious of it.

She became nervous as her time approached. 'Thank the Lord that you will be here still, that you will not be gone to sea.'

'You are a sailor's wife, you must know how to do without me.'

'Not for this. For this I want to know that you are here.'

'It is your doing, not mine. I can be of no assistance.' So vulnerable she looked when he said that, but he was out of his depth. 'I am a man, you understand. I know nothing of all this.'

He wished she would not make this demand which was beyond him.

'Well, I can call on Kirsten Pedersdatter if you like, if it is necessary.'

And he went to see Mistress Pedersdatter that same day and she gave him herbs to calm her, and when he asked if there was not something else, she gave him also a strange white stone that Johanne must wear on a string about her neck. It was egglike and rattled as if it had a loose piece inside and she said that it came from an eagle's nest. He paid much for the stone and did not know if his money was well spent. She took the coins in her clean white hands and smiled then to assure him that the words to follow came free of charge. Her smile was odd because of the length of her teeth in her narrow face, as if she was a very old horse, but her eyes were warm as chestnuts. 'See that she eats well. You don't want to have her pine away. See if you cannot get her some good greens, the darker the better, and red meat, liver; such dark foods will make her strong.'

'Will you come to visit her? You could speak to her and that I'm sure would help.'

'You would be wasting your money to have me there now. Wait and have me when you need me.'

And he went back to Johanne and she prepared her own tisanes, and he bought food at the market and she cooked it.

What she needed was a woman, he saw, and felt then brutish and inadequate. Hans Jakobsen, though he was so talkative in his shop, was silent at home, far away. He tried to ask Johanne once if it had always been so, if her father had always sat like that at nights, silent in his chair, and let her play her games about him, even when she was small. Johanne had looked puzzled at his question and said of course, but wasn't it always thus, didn't every man like thus to quietly mull over all the words of the working day? So that, he saw, was how she had learnt the stillness of her evenings, those long evenings when she rustled and stitched and moved only to feed the fire; how she had learnt the appearance of self-reliance that, in all but this question of her pregnancy, gave her a presence beyond her years.

'Stay with me.'

He was about to go out, to the market and to the harbour. He had his hat and coat on and was tying his boots. That memorable winter had not let up although it was February; the cold had seemed only to intensify with the winds that swept in on them these last few days from the Baltic, that howled in from iron skies and drove even the skaters away indoors.

'Please stay.'

'Come on, girl. I'll only be a short time. And your father's in the shop.'

She was looking pale, now he thought of it, but that might be due only to the biting cold, which whistled in through the cracks in the shutters and through the door as he opened it.

When he came back she was leaning forwards across the

bed, her face held in tightened hands, heaving with silenced pain. He dropped his things and went to her but could not touch her; a person in pain is so alone. He held her only when the spasm was gone.

It was too soon, she said. She knew that something was not right. Kirsten Pedersdatter had told her the day to expect, the time of the moon.

'You cannot be sure, Mistress Pedersdatter could be wrong. She is no physician after all.'

'No physician, but people about here say that she has more knowledge than any Latin-speaking doctor of medicine in all of Copenhagen.'

In the pause before the next pain came they prayed together. And when she rose from her knees he wrapped her shawl about her, placed pillows on the bed, made her comfortable as he could. He made to go downstairs to prepare a tisane but she would not let him at first, would not let him leave her alone in the room. He had to tear her hands from him and hold them by her sides before he could free himself from her, and then he went down and called to Hans, and went to the neighbouring women's houses to get them to come and help, and once they were with her and there seemed to be some relief or at least a pattern to the pains, he went out and walked a long way through iced and empty streets.

He had no sense of how long he was gone. There was little enough light in the sky, less to penetrate the narrow gap between the old houses that leaned towards one another overhead. The darkening of the end of day was scarcely perceptible save in the intensifying glow of candles and firelight from the windows he passed. He walked slowly, watching the ground, for the dark ice was deceptive and it was easy to slip. Once or twice he hovered before the rumble of noise from an inn or beer cellar. The idea of warmth enticed him, the thought of a shot of liquor spreading its warmth inside him, but each time he drew back thinking that he could not take the press of people. Such a crush of men you found in a bar, such brightness of face and voice. He was not a man for crowds, he had spent too much of his life apart from them and his soul needed space about it. So he walked to the water. That was what one did in that crowded city, one walked to the water for calm. He walked north until he had reached the ramparts and put all the houses behind him, and stood at the edge and gazed into space, a long view out beyond ice-bound ships into the blankness that had been sea, stood and thought until the wind cut through to his bones, and only then turned back, guilty for the stolen time.

When he came to the midwife's house he knocked at the door, and waited a long time until he heard a clatter on the stairs inside and a younger woman came and answered who he saw must be Kirsten Pedersdatter's daughter, so like her she was, only younger and her face a little plumper, more flesh about the teeth.

'My name is Thomas Cave. My wife is in urgent need of your mother, at least I guess that Mistress Pedersdatter is your mother.' The likeness in the young woman's face was so complete that he wondered that any father, any man, could have had a part in the making of her.

'My mother is out. She was called away.'

'Will you tell her then soon as she comes back?'

'I cannot say when that will be.'

'Tell her anyway. Tell her we need her to come.' Almost he had asked the daughter to come instead, as if she must have inherited her mother's cunning along with her features.

'Wait one moment.' She left him standing at the door and disappeared down the dark passage that ran beside the stairs, came back a few minutes later with something in her hand. 'I think she would give you this for your wife.'

'What is it?

'For the pain. If it becomes very bad.'

The faces of the women at the house barely registered his return. He felt that they did not care that he had been gone or for how long, as if he was quite irrelevant to the event. Only Johanne wished to see him. She was walking about the room, her face taut, a glitter in her eyes.

She put out a hand to him. 'You went out. I told you not to go.'

'I went to look for Mistress Pedersdatter.'

'You were gone such a long time.'

'It is the state you are in, my dear, that makes a few minutes seem like an hour.'

At that moment a wave of pain broke in her and she gasped and bent forward across the bed and held her weight up on clenched fists that dug into the covers. She did not speak again until it had receded.

'Where is she then?'

Kirsten Pedersdatter did not come until after midnight. There was no sleep in the house save for the apprentice up in the attic. Hans had kept up in his shop working in a fixed silence that he did not break even when he unlocked the door to her. He made no acknowledgement that he knew either her or the cause of her coming, but let her pass him and go to Cave who had descended the stairs at her knock.

'At last,' said Thomas Cave. 'You said you would come when she needed you. What kept you?'

She did not bother to reply. Her lips pursed over her teeth and the look in her eyes was too sharp for him. She told him to make the women who were watching go. And when they were alone, she had Johanne lie on her back on the floor where she could handle her most easily and pulled up her nightgown to expose the great pained whale of her belly. She knelt then beside her and with those pale hands felt her systematically, prodded and pressed, spread her legs wide and folded them up and felt between them.

'I thought so. I thought it was too soon. It is far sooner than it should be. I do not know why it has started now.'

'What can you do?'

'I? I can do little but wait, like you. And tell her also to wait, to be patient. Have her waters gone?'

'No. Nothing has occurred but the pain.'

'Then there is still a chance that this may settle. The baby is the wrong way up, and too high in her. Perhaps I could give her belladonna to still the spasms and that would give more time for it to move.'

'Do that then.'

'Wait. Not so urgent. I will watch awhile, I will see how it is going.'

And she told him to sleep and he went to sleep in the room next to that one which was Hans's room, and as he left he saw her go down on the floor again and press and pummel with her strong white hands, and heard her begin to speak some long spiel in a rhythmic undertone whose words he could not catch.

He must have gone to sleep still listening to it because when he woke the first thing he noticed was the silence in the house. There was not a sound from her room, barely a sound from the sleeping city save for the clock chimes and the early cockerels. Hans slept on the bed beside him: so he had at last put away his work and pulled himself upstairs, and Thomas Cave had been unconscious of his coming. There was grey light enough to make out his form, scrunched to the side with the blanket pulled over and one thin leg bent from it, shuddering slightly with his exhalations of breath. When a dog barked somewhere close to the house he rolled over and began to snore, a soft rattling snore, as another dog took up the call and a wave of barking spread through the district. Thomas Cave took himself up then, gentle beside the other man, and creaked through to the room where the women waited.

Kirsten Pedersdatter sat in an upright chair close to the

107

window, arms dangling, body limp as if she slept but her eyes open, watching. Her patient lay on the bed now, coiled as far as her bulk would allow her. He could not see if she was asleep or awake, and before he could come closer Kirsten Pedersdatter put a finger to her lips and led him out to the landing and down the stairs.

In the thin daylight of the parlour below she spoke.

'I have given her something to help her sleep a little. She is going to need all the strength that God can give her.'

It had begun, she said, not as childbirth but as a disturbance of the womb. She could not tell the cause but looked out where the last star faded and the sun rose between the roofs in a painful streak of pink. She shrugged: God's will; an evil eye.

'Or just luck,' said Thomas Cave. 'Chance? Or the way she is made, some inherited feature like that hair of hers or her blue eyes, but this a flaw, some flaw in her body passed down from her mother? Did you know that her mother died at her birth?'

'I know because I was there. But be reassured, it was not like this, it was not the same.'

For five days it went on. The pains came and racked her and she gasped and screamed cat's screams, and sometimes she would growl and bite on a piece of leather he brought up from the shop downstairs, thick hide that she gnawed through with her teeth and clenched and kneaded with her hands. In the intervals she breathed with deliberation to quell the whimpers and then sought him with her eyes. And then he looked into them and saw a calm deep inside her and thought of a madonna with dark-gold hair tumbling about a face of childish innocence.

'Will you play for me, Thomas?'

He took his fiddle down and played a sad slow tune that he knew, played at first as delicately as he knew how, but then he saw that any kind of music affected her and began to play the most unlikely things: dance tunes, church tunes, the banging rhythms of bawdy songs, anything at all with sound to draw her away from her sensation. He was a scratcher at the fiddle, no musician worth the name; if he played for others he played for them to dance and drink and sing, not for listening. He had no subtlety. Yet here in the small upstairs room before the bed he played and lost himself in it, and for moments she was lost in it too, and there were moments when the other women were there that from the atmosphere it might have seemed a celebration instead of what it was.

Each day, once or twice, Kirsten Pedersdatter came by, came without speaking through the shop, where still Hans did not appear to see her though Cave knew by her word that she had attended on his own wife's fatal confinement, and went up to Johanne, and felt and pummelled and put her ear to her great drum of a belly to listen for the baby's heart, put her fingers inside the woman to measure how far she was open, put her hand to her head to feel its heat, looked at her eyes that were mapped with red veins from the straining. Thomas and the women stood back when she came, sometimes leaving the room and sometimes watching from a distance, and she did not speak to them at all and barely even to her patient, though she muttered frequently under her breath, sometimes at such extended length that he believed she spoke some incantation. Once she brought something and tied it about her middle beneath her clothing, and when the women looked at it later they said that it was the skin of a snake.

He took courage towards the end and followed her into the street. How it dazzled him; he had not been out for days and there was sun trying to break through the sea fog.

She looked at him with eyes hard as little nuts.

'Your wife is very weak. The pain has drained all her strength.'

'Is there nothing you can do?'

'You have seen that I do all I can.'

'At least, can you give her something else for the pain?'

'The drugs she has had already are strong. They cannot be taken for much longer without becoming killers themselves.'

11

I THINK I HAVE not seen here in Greenland – if this island, as I now know it to be, be indeed Greenland – snow of the gentle kind we have in our southern latitude. What snow there is, in the depths of this unforgiving winter, is a hard, mean, constipated snow that swirls about in the wind and strikes like pinpricks on any little patch of eyelid or other exposed skin. Three days ago I killed a bear, praise be to God for His care of me in this wilderness, a kill in which I had much luck, the bear being caught astride a steep slope so that though the range was not close a single shot sufficed to knock him down and disable him. Only that the place was distant from my cabin and it has taken all of these past days to skin and butcher him and bring in the pieces to hang, the chore performed in stages as my gloveless fingers became bitten with the cold. Were it not for the new meat my spirits would be very low. There is great anxiety in these interminable days of half-light and spitting snow.

★　　★　　★

The snow that last day fell so softly, he remembered, that he had thought it a sign that God had relented. What would he not give, in this hard place, for snow like that? From dawn onwards it fell, light and thick at the same time, and covered the filthy ice and the stained drifts about the streets with a thick white down, and when he went out he had turned up his face to feel the flakes drop like feathers against it and slip away, felt some of them catch and thaw in the crack between his lips. The chilling easterly had dropped, the temperature perceptibly lifted, and he knew that this snow would not last with them as the earlier snows of that winter had done, but cover only for a brief time and melt away, and that there was every chance that the sun would come in its wake. He had a sense of all the warmth and light of the sun being there but only waiting behind the softness of the snowcloud.

He went to find the Pastor. As he felt the kindness of the snow on him he wondered if it was any longer necessary. The women had pressed him to it and for a time he had resisted. 'See, she is in agony,' they said. 'She is too weak, she will never push it out.' There were so many visiting women, so many voices who knew what he did not. 'She will tear,' said an old woman, some thin crone from up the street on whom he had never set eyes before: 'It will tear her apart from the inside.' Even good Anna Nielsdatter, the baker's wife, who had looked after Johanne often when she was a child: 'I have borne seventeen children, two sets of twins, six stillborn, and I have never known a birth like this.' So many voices at him and yet he did not act until she herself asked and he saw that her hope was almost gone.

The snow clung to the tower of the church, lodged in the

carvings of the stones in the churchyard. It lay on the black brim of the Pastor's hat and in the folds of his cloak as he walked. It fell like petals outside the window of her room so that when he called her to consciousness that the Pastor was there she asked suddenly if the cherry tree beyond the wall was in flower.

And they knelt in the room and spoke prayers and the Pastor read from the Bible. The door opened and people came and went as they prayed, and when he looked round he saw that Kirsten Pedersdatter knelt among them and the daughter who looked like her beside her, and did not know why it was that he was surprised to see them.

When the Pastor left most of the women left with him, going out and down the narrow stairs with a steady rustle of skirts like a procession. The grey room seemed to settle behind them as if it was cleared of more than their presence, as if it was cleared of action, of effort and fear, all the air in it exhausted and exhaled. Only Kirsten Pedersdatter and her daughter remained besides himself and Hans, who had left his tools at last to take up a place at the bedside.

'Thank you, Mistress Pedersdatter, for all you have done. I know that you have great skill and have worked hard. Whatever comes to pass is no more than God's will.' In his new resignation he felt that he must settle with her, thank and straighten accounts.

'Wait. One thing, there is just one thing. If you will allow me, there is perhaps one last thing more that we may do.'

Insistent voice, insistent eyes. As she spoke the spasms racked through Johanne's body again and he did not know that he could bear any more, let alone that she could.

'My daughter has brought me a drug that was prepared by a friend, a woman who has taught me much. It might yet give her the strength to expel the child that I know still lives inside her.' Her words were like a drum to his head. Her mirror-daughter stood beside her, doubling her persuasion. 'I know that it lives, I have heard its heartbeat, weak but still there. It is a strong child and she is a strong woman. Let me try this, I ask you.' And she brought out from a cloth bag her daughter handed her a small phial of blue glass. 'I cannot say for sure what it will do, only that I trust the woman who made it more than I trust myself.'

More hope, more pain. His mind reeled. He looked across the bed to Hans but never had he seen that intent and expressive face so closed, absent to him. He looked outside. The snow outside fell so softly, covering, blanketing everything, as if no more effort should be made, as if everything should be blanketed in its soft white cover.

He thinks now that hope hurts more than anything.

These days of false dawns have been anguish to him. He has woken to the beginning of light, to a pinkness in the southern sky that has spread itself and crept about the entire horizon, all about his vision, the pinkness of a sun about to rise that holds him expectant through all the hours of a day and then fades and leaves him cheated. At the time that he must imagine to be midday he has seen brightness and shadow move high on the mountains to the south of the island as the light of a hidden sun passes across them. At that same hour for each of the past three days he has climbed the mountain at the end of the beach and looked, and he has thought he has seen the tip of the yellow disc of the sun on the horizon, only to have it flicker and waver like a mirage and disappear. Now again he fights his way up the mountainside, fights because of the wind that has arisen, cold as any wind he has known in this desolate place, which comes again and again in icy gusts and tries to push him down. He climbs bent low so that he is not caught in the full force of it and blown away, and when he nears the top finds that he must crawl on hands and knees and at last lie flat on the rock that the wind has bared of snow.

He sees the mountains laid out, the crumpled ice of the bay and the fjord, the mountains of the land on the other side, and far away, the vague stillness of the frozen ocean. Everything has faint colour, the pinkness of the sky everywhere reflected, the shadows lilac, all quite unreal. For a second he thinks he does at last see the sun, forming all at once yellow and round distinctly above the horizon and separated from it, and then remembers that that is not at all how the sun appears and understands that this again can only be a mirage.

Is it the wind or is it the despair in him that whips tears to his eyes and clouds his vision? A blue bottle: more pain. Why did he let them give it to her? He lets himself stand in the wind and a great gust takes him and blows him away. For an instant he is blown into air as if he might fly, and then he crashes down on his shoulder, his hip, his head, crashes and rolls down the mountainside, his limbs thrown about him. Some great distance he falls, he knows only the sensation and the pain, and then, with sudden extreme awareness, knows that an avalanche has begun to fall with him. So, he knows it now: he is gone, he will be buried spread flat as he is upon the snow, the mountain itself will bury him where there is no man to do it. And yet he continues to fall and the snow covers him no deeper than a spray flying back across his body, and he realises that it is carrying him. He is being carried on the surface of the avalanche like a raft on rapids, the current tossing and throwing him but all the while rushing him down. Lord, if only there is no rock. If only this will end without a rock. And at last, with surprising softness, he finds that he has come to rest. He opens his eyes to the merciful snow heaped beneath him and to the lilac sky. How far he has fallen and yet he is still alive. He had not thought it possible. The Shepherd gathers his lost sheep and saves them from harm. Slowly he picks himself up, almost as if he must gather the pieces of himself together, as if he is not sure that they will fit together again. His head has taken a sharp blow: he can feel the swelling on it, the blood in his matted hair. He has pains too in his shoulder where his weight first fell, in his ankle and in his chest. He speaks to himself, would speak aloud if the cold had not contracted his lips and reduced his voice to a ventriloquist's whisper. Slowly now, Thomas Cave. Have patience, man, have care. Hold to the sober way you have always lived, one step at a time, never giving way to emotion or despair. The Lord has brought you this far; now it is to yourself to bring yourself in. You yourself are your own witness as much as the Lord. You know your strength, your weakness. By discipline, by reason and by care, you can control the means of your survival.

116

Each step he takes hurts him. He counts five, then stops, falls to the ground and lies there without sense of time. No good, he tells himself, that is not how you save yourself. Keep count, keep track. You have not been here all these months to let go now. Pick yourself up again, you did it before. Again, five steps. A pause. Five more and he leans on a rock to catch his breath. Stabs of pain in his shoulder and his ankle, yet the ankle will just take his weight. Next time he forces himself to a dozen steps and rests standing on his good leg. In this way, stage by stage, he makes his way back to the tent.

He sees the child at once, lit in the glow from the stove. A baby asleep. It sleeps with that serenity seen only in the very young, such trust in the smoothness of the closed eyelids, the curl of the lashes, the faint curl of a mouth that smiles in a dream. It is plump and warm, the shawl in which it is wrapped loose about it, basking in a warmth that he enveloped in all his furs can scarcely imagine. Can this be his son? For the first time he knows what it is to have a living son. He kneels down, takes in the pinkness of the boy's cheeks, the softness of his skin, his round arms, his little loosely clenched fists, the dark-gold curls beneath his cap. He removes a glove and understands that even the most tender touch would burn like ice on that little coiled hand that seems to reach out to him.

What if he were to touch him? Would he wake and cry, a boy's lusty cry to fill the cabin, or would he disappear? He reaches out in wonder and in horror, holds his fingers an inch away; their tips can sense the warmth that comes off a sleeping body. If this is a hallucination, he could not have believed one could be so complete, so warm, so alive. Even she did not come so alive to him.

12

H E S I T S C L O S E to the fire as he can be, closes his eyes
in his reeling head. Slowly, as the heat penetrates, he
begins to distinguish the separate pains. He sees that he must
be thankful. He was lucky, or blessed, to be caught so in the
white hands of the snow. His ankle pains him badly. It is
blinding torture to take off his boot but when he examines
the injury he is reassured to see that the joint bends this way
and that as far as its swelling will allow and he believes that he
will be able to walk on it again before too long. The colour
of the bruising is already violent and he can imagine it will be
as bad on his back and on his ribs though he has not stripped
himself of his clothing which belongs on him now like a
matted extra skin. How much worse it could have been.
With much discomfort he kneels to pray, thanks God for his
deliverance. And then he tries to find an easy position on the
cot and attempts to rest. The silence in the cabin is suddenly
so complete that he believes that the wind outside has
entirely dropped.

It is only a short time before he compels himself to move again, flexes his stiffening body and his ankle in an attempt to keep them supple. He finds himself a stick of a good size and hobbles across the room, hobbles even to the outer door of the tent to see.

This night the lights have shot across the sky in the most terrible manner, like as the world was bound to end or as if it had ended already in all places but here. It was as if I might have seen in the heavens the reflection of a distant battle, the flames, the palls of smoke, the arcs of gunfire, all reversed and distorted and discoloured into faint and indescribable shades of green and rose, orange and violet, all the violent sound of it reduced at this great distance to a whirring like that of spinning wings.

In truth it was only a hint of a sound, a whirring or whistling so faint that he did not know if it was in his head or outside of it, and beneath its strange high hum he seemed to hear a softer tone, a contralto murmur that came and went like waves. It sounded like a voice, a woman's voice, her voice soothing the child: a lullaby sung beneath the breath in that language of hers that was so plain and bare to feeling.

He thinks that he does not sleep more than a moment for all the throbbing of his body and his brain. He does not even attempt sleep for most of that night but sits up at the table in the lamplight as he had in the early days and engrosses himself in his work, chipping away persistently and mechanically as if by doing so he might make his mind inert as the materials he handles, dull the pictures in it, make it plain, true, predictable as wood and metal.

The picture of Johanne, laid out, hair spread on to her shoulders. Once the agony was over her face was calm and he knew her again. And even as he did he wondered how far he had ever known her when he could not begin to understand what had passed inside, as if she had only ever been an idea to him, a dream, a surface, a texture, not herself but a face, a girl, a wife.

She was never so real as what is in his hands. Wood, metal. These things he can know. Not those others.

Not that creature beside her. He had them cover it so that he did not have to see.

This work he can do without thinking now, he could shape heels with his eyes closed. To better engage his mind he has thought to make himself a pair of clogs: the bases hollowed out of wood, warm on the cold ground; the uppers of sealskin, well-oiled and with the fur turned outwards as he has seen on the boots of Lappish traders. He has found a block of beech from off the ship that will serve well, has taken some sealskin, scraped and steeped it until it is supple.

The indentation of the sole, the rise of the instep; it is true what Hans had told him, that he has an instinct for the craft. They might have worked well together if he had stayed. They might have expanded the shop to serve the gentry, taken on another boy or two, hired a servant to greet the ladies: Jakobsen and Cave, shoemakers of Copenhagen.

121

Only he knew, knew as clear as if he had already lived it, what sort of life that would have been. The hollowness of it, that set a terrible silent clamour echoing within him. People all around, and the absence of them inside. The faces of the fashionable like masks; the faces of all, eyes, smiles, voices, false and alien to him. The city in which he had thought to find a home as alien without her as any place that he had ever been to, any place where he had come to shore with sea-worn eyes out of focus; all its acquired familiarity, its houses, its spires, its known sights, no more than things he might at some distant time have been shown a picture of or imagined in a dream.

And yet he had stayed some weeks, two, three months, without the impulse to move. He had stayed at first as he must to see them buried in the graveyard, mother and child-that-had-not-been, the two in one coffin as if the instant of separation had never occurred, the one name upon the stone.

Stay, said Hans. In the day, in the shop with work before them, it was well. What he could not bear was the quiet in the evening.

He saw the whaleships leave harbour at the start of the season, the *Gabriel* on which he had sailed the year before. He had refused his place on her yet when he saw her go he suddenly envied the look of her, sailing out on a fresh breeze one April morning when all the roofs and towers of the city glowed bright behind. It seemed brave on such a fine spring day to sail out towards the ice when there on the land the grass began to ripple in the meadows and the blossom blew off the trees. He watched until she was gone from the horizon and knew that before long, somehow, he also would be gone.

The next ship that would take him was a cargo ship bound for the Shetlands. He did not care where she went. Swiftly he took his leave, took with him in addition to what he had come with only a shawl that Johanne had embroidered, of fine creamy wool patterned with coloured threads, and this he used to wrap his violin. He wrapped the instrument with care though he had not played it since those strange days in the upstairs room, took not a note from it as he folded it in the wool, and the bow beside it, and packed it at the top of his chest. He could find no suitable words with which to part from Hans Jakobsen, who had closed his shop and had the apprentice help him all the way to the dock to see him leave. So long as I remain there is place for you here, Hans told him, and it was pathetic to see him lean so on the dull boy's shoulders.

Good Hans. Goodbye Hans. He could explain nothing.

There was no one else from whom he felt the need to take his leave. None on the new ship would know that the English sailor they took on board had any more than a passing connection with the city nor any but the most elementary knowledge of the Danish language.

They made it quickly to Lerwick, the same fair gale behind them all the way, a quick, fresh voyage that whipped life into his cheeks if not into his soul. The Shetlands seemed nowhere: plain, bare islands beaten by the sea and suited to his mood. He left the Danish ship, took his chest and went ashore. He found lodging at an inn. Those he met there asked how long he would stay but he answered only an indefinite time, as if he were waiting for something to occur. He had there an attic room with a high view out over the harbour to the sea, and a number of times each day, so many repeated minutes he could not add and count them, he stood with his long back bent beneath the slope of the roof and looked into the grey distance, feeling inside himself that same blank boredom that he had known on the longest voyages. It was, he thought, the way a man feels when he has been gone so long from the point of departure that the purpose of a journey is lost and with it all sense of the possibility of arrival.

There were many ships that passed across his view. He observed their passage in and out the harbour with no more interest than if they had been driftwood on the sea. He could barely have said which was coming and which going, let alone which way they were headed. He must have seen the *Heartsease* coming in from the south, a sturdy three-masted bark, seventy tons, nothing special about her, no particular reason he should note her. There were other English ships, other whalers even, putting in for water and last supplies before the final haul north.

A shaft of sun was all it took, breaking the clouds. He was standing idle by the harbour, and there was a brilliant shaft of sunlight and into it stepped the figure of Captain Marmaduke. Then he knew the energy of the black-haired Captain, the force of his smile. We're short a man. The firmness of his handshake.

Two days later he was high in the rigging of the *Heartsease* with the scream of gulls about him. He saw the rocky island recede and marvelled that it could remain so fixed with all the winds and tides and currents that pressed upon it.

How good it had been at first to come again to the briskness of the North. Somewhere hard and cold. Somewhere that had no memory. No history of man. Or woman.

Such crispness there was on that ship. She had been held some days before the Scottish coast, made it late to Shetland and now on the voyage north she sped to make up the lost time. He had heard the name of Captain Thomas Marmaduke even in the Danish ports, and was impressed to see the boldness of the man and his sureness of the Greenland seas. He took them further than any of the whalers of the Companies, beyond the scope of charts, east and beyond where only Barents was known to have been, up a wide fjord where the ice had only just broken up and to the great bay that came to be called Duke's Cove, to which he had led a trio of Hull ships the previous year. The crew were mostly Hull men with open faces and heavy voices, save for the Biscayans who did the skilled whaling work and who were dark and popish and crossed themselves for fear and luck and when they woke in the morning and before they slept.

They got to the bay not a day too soon, for they found that it was already filling with whales. Great herds of them came in to breed at that time of year as the thaw set in and the ice in the sea cracked and broke apart and made a passage through. The ship went in and waited, and the great unsuspecting beasts frolicked in with spouts and grand slaps of their tails as if they gathered to play at a fairground there among the ice.

No fog those first few days and he was light-headed with the brightness and the present moment. It was when they began the hunting that his mood began to change.

Thomas Cave had been whaling before but never till now had he seen it like this. That winter ashore had marked him and put him at a distance from men. He saw his fellows with a strange objectivity as they went about their work, as if he saw them, and himself also, from a distance and without connection. He saw the hugeness of the landscape and of the whales, how small the men and their boats were beside them, small as if they could be picked up and crumpled in God's hand. He saw the dark Biscayans with their harpoons, like pictures he had seen of little devils with their forks, and he saw the leviathans slaughtered; saw, with a strange and dawning horror, the whirlpools about them, the streaming wakes of their flight, the red fountains of blood that spouted up as they died, then the great red stain that spread across the bay, heavy with blubber-oil and the debris of death, and slapped against the ship's side, and the screeching hordes of gulls that dived amongst it. It came to him like an image almost of hell. He saw it and yet he worked on at the heart of the thing, worked on the carcases that they brought in and tied to the side of the ship, climbed the slippery, lice-encrusted bodies and cut the blubber off them. He worked through bright day and light night. He talked little to the others of the crew. When the work stopped and they went

126

on shore, he brushed by them in silence. They sat before a fire and ate the rich whale and walrus meat and drank their ale and talked and swore, but Thomas Cave sat apart.

There was a lad of fourteen who made them laugh, a fresh-faced boy still with a touch of the land to him, who could as well have been an acrobat as come to sea, who somersaulted and turned cartwheels and tumbled before them. He would turn himself over a half-dozen times and land on his hands instead of his feet and walk away like that with his feet in the air and his hair down over his face, or bend his body back so that he was like a crab and scuttle sidelong down to the water's edge, then back up again and turn his head and grin upside-down at the man who stood above him.

'Would you catch a crab, sir?'

Cave did not joke but only shook his head, and the boy sprang upright again, for he was a kind boy and was sobered by an intuition of the sadness in him.

'My name is Thomas Goodlard, I think we have not spoken before. I've been working on one of the whaleboats. It's my first time out.'

'And what do you think of it?'

'It's hard, isn't it, but grand?' The boy was like a puppy and could not sit still. 'Like it's all new and there's no past here and everything's still to happen. I never imagined there could be a place in the world like this.'

Thomas Cave heard the East Anglian inflection in the boy's voice, looked about him at the other men, at the oddity of the gathering on the beach, at the mountains that stood so cold and serene above them in the light of the night. He saw that the boy was wrong: each man before the fire had brought his past with him, a history there whether it was wanted or not, in each face and each voice, and he realised that even here where there were none to remind him he would not forget. He understood that she had come to Greenland with him.

He works the night through. He has gouged out from the wood the shape of his foot, curved the ends of it so that it will roll beneath his step. He takes up a second piece of beech and begins the reverse form for the other foot. Every now and then he makes a test, turns quickly in case she is there in the corner of his eye. Can she really have gone? Was it not just now, this same night, that he saw her out there beneath those whirring lights, walking in the snow with the child on her hip, singing to him?

'This is no place for you. Nor for him most of all. Go back, go away! Why do you bring him here?'

It was she. He could have sworn that it was she. A shawl drawn about the child and over her head so that it hid her face, but he knew her by the way she stood, with a gentle weight as if she had spread roots into the white ground. She stood quite still, some few yards off, and a sudden gust of wind blew specks of snow on to the curve of her head and shoulders and into the folds of the shawl. She did not lift her head to look at him but when he shouted her song stopped, the hum of the lullaby she had been singing.

'Do you hear me? Go, in God's Name. Whatever kind of

apparition you are, and I know that you are not Johanne, go.' Each word hurt him as he spoke it.

Still she stood, still as a statue. Then at last she brushed away the snow that had gathered on her shawl and rearranged it, wrapping its end tighter about the child that clung to her side, and when she had finished she took up another song, a livelier song this one, in a stronger tone that carried well against the wind. A Danish song; he could not make out the words but it was jaunty like a nursery rhyme or a playground chant. Again she wrapped the shawl and began to turn away, rocking the little boy on her hip to the rhythm of the song, and the little boy pushed back the shawl so that he saw him for the first time, and put out his head and beat his round fist against her chest and began to laugh.

How long ago had it been? Ten minutes, an hour? The work before him, the work that he has done this night, suggests that it was longer, the surface of the table and the floor about him a curling sea of wooden parings. He feels the chisel in his hand, how his palm is pressed into its shape, has been clenched about it for so long that it is hard to loosen his fingers and release the wood. Yet he puts the tool down and stretches out his hand, and as he does so his own cruel shouts reverberate the louder in his brain.

'Go, go, go!' he called into the wind, and the song still came back to him though he could see them no longer.

'Be gone!'

He sank down then on his knees on the polished crust of ice before the door of the tent and began to pray, formlessly at first, stuttering 'Our Fathers', holding and re-uttering random phrases as if the simple repetition of church words was effective incantation. Then the tears came slowly and froze on his beard and he began to speak what he knew of the service of burial. Let him bury them, bury them again, bury even their memory in the snow. Let there be no more dreams, no more ghosts, no more of superstition. Let there be no more before him than what he knows by his reason, the hard evidence of the material world. Let survival be his sole intent. Ashes to ashes, ice to ice. His breathing had soothed with the order of the words, and the luminosity of the sky faded until there was only a blink of green in the stars above the horizon, and the night became densely black but he could not believe that she was gone.

'Go, God damn you! Go to the Devil. I will not have you here!'

13

'*T*RULY THE LIGHT *is sweet, and a pleasant thing it is for the eyes to behold the sun.' I have read again on this twenty-seventh day of February the lines of Ecclesiastes, and never I believe did any man since the Testament was written know the sun so gloriously resurrected.*

I do not know on which day I might first have seen it from my vantage point on the mountain. I have not been able to climb again all these past days on account of my injury. All this week I have had the sense of the sun's closeness, the weather each morning clear and full of promise, the colours of the sunrise holding in the sky the full length of a day, the light falling gold and pink on the ice, and this light becoming so directional at noontime, gilding the mountaintops and throwing their shadows across the clefts behind them, that I must conclude that its orb would already have been visible from the heights. Down here where my cabin lies, just a little above the level of the frozen sea, where I hobble about my tasks with a crutch made up out of whalebone and my ankle, which remains too swollen to fit into a boot, swaddled in bearskin, I saw not even a slice of it until this day.

And then seeing it I left my work, and it drew me, hobbling down the hard path my movements have beaten into the snow, down to the edge of the land and out some short distance on to the ice of the bay where the widest view may be obtained of the southern horizon.

Never has a sight been more welcome, never surely more beautiful: the rosy sky, the soft streaks of yellow in it, the glow that lit from below the few skimming clouds, the sun itself, and all that reflected again on the ice below. My words cannot begin to convey my elation at that moment, my exhilaration that the predicted and sure event in which yet at the darkest moments I had almost ceased to believe, had finally come to pass, my tearful relief which must have been akin to that of the women who saw the stone rolled back and met a living man in the Garden of the Tomb.

The vision was over within minutes, the sun slipping away as eerily as it had come, down behind the curvature of the Earth. And when it had gone the relief burst out in him, and he spread his legs and dug his crutch in firm, took in a great breath and cried out, a great resounding holler fit to shatter all the ice.

And then.

Thomas Cave puts down his pen and reads back what he has written. There is falseness in the words, but does the falseness lie in them or between them? Writing, like speech, is part performance and even when it is true it is not the truth. For he has not written all of it. He will not write the all of it. How the cry died. How the last echo faded off the land behind him as the colours left the sky. How elation turned, and faith was no longer there. How he wept again then, wept on and on, a crumpled man.

He wept until the tears were ice.

And then at last he picked up his crutch and hobbled back, and the pain in his ankle as he put his weight on it was the one vivid point in all the emptiness around and within him.

Fool, he tells himself. Foolish Cave, you should have known. The light of the sun is not spring. Winter is not done with you yet. Survival does not lie in the heavens but in a man's patience, above all.

Even when the darkness was at its worst he had not known such bleak monotony as comes to him during these last months of the winter. The days stretch, each one of them almost tangibly longer than the last, but they do not warm. The equinox comes and is passed, a day of such cold uniform light that almost he wishes to have the dark back. That his soul may sleep, that the sun had not come to wake it. That he might but lie down on the ice through the empty day and sleep.

April first. I record here that according to my calendar March has run into April, yet still there is no change save for this lengthening of the light. Can this indeed be April? Such hope in the word as I have always known it, joy and spring and the rise of sap there just in the word alone, but here in this place it is not any April deserving of the name.

I live. I have food for some weeks more. The days grow, but that is all. Time is barren. I have determined that I shall cease from writing until life stirs inside it.

14

WHITE ON WHITE.

The fox is hard to see even three yards off, just a
ripple of white in all the white as it searches through the
snow-covered heap of bones and scraps that has grown all
winter outside the tent. Thomas Cave constructs a trap like
those he has made in the past for shipboard rats, using split
scrimshaw whalebone that is strong but fine and flexible and
springy, baits it with pieces of meat gone rancid in his store.

The fox was hungry. Next morning it is caught. He hangs
it to freeze and dry three days in the biting wind and cooks it
then with plums and raisins. He takes up his log once more
and records the act, and the flavour of the meat. *The meat of
the white fox is sinewy and strong, a rough meat but fresh.*

A flutter of white is a bird in the snow. It is so long since
he has seen a bird. He knows it as a ptarmigan, recognises
now its odd rattling call. He has heard this sound off and on
for days, a sound that is almost mechanical and that has made
him look over his shoulder and unnerved him. Strange soft

white bird, so comfortable it looks on the snow. When it is still, only the line of black that runs from its eye to its beak betrays it. Though he has his musket in his hand he does not take it up to aim. There is too much promise in the sight.

He begins to see bears frequently now, coming close up to the tent but also in the distance as they cross the ice, the more easily distinguishable as their fur shows stained and yellowish on bright days against the snow. There are lone bears but often pairs, mothers with their cubs, and when he hunts and kills a mother he is both astonished and distressed to see the devotion with which the cub stays by and must be killed itself rather than leave its mother's side. Over the course of the winter he has developed an admiration for these beasts which the harshest conditions do not deter, and which seem to roam so far and wide, appearing sometimes from across the ice as if they have skated across oceans to reach the island. He sees that they move on the ice like skaters, with long slipping steps, and as the ice begins to melt he is amazed to observe how light they can be in motion, escaping his gun at times by cutting across ice far thinner than he himself would dare to walk on.

At last the thaw becomes a perceptible process although there are days still, sometimes a week together, of blizzard and cold equal to any that he has previously experienced. It is the sky that first tells him that the ice has begun to break up out beyond the bay, dark streaks of what Captain Duke had called water sky, revealing by the intensity of its reflected colour wherever the darkness of clear sea, rather than the paleness of ice, lies beneath. Out there it is evident also that the sea has begun to move, for daily he witnesses the effects of the tide as its flow and ebb varies the pressure on the ice in the bay and causes it to creak and move and in places to crack open. He sees that ice rots before it dissolves, its texture becoming soft and spongy before it disintegrates into porridge and slush. Where it breaks and pools are revealed, the exposed sea reeks steam into the sunlight as if it had boiled beneath.

With the melt a drab and dirty world which he had almost forgotten begins to re-emerge. There is seaweed, slimy and almost black in colour, which the bears claw up on the strand, and patches of anaemic moss. There is the carcase of a fox that must have frozen as the winter began and become buried in the snow. In the area around the tent the objects of the whale station once more show themselves, and also his own detritus: not only the bones and scraps but every sausage of faeces he has carried out that winter and dumped beside the path. He begins to be aware now as he approaches his lodging of its smell, a smell that has become a constant of his enclosed existence, a fetid and manly smell of smoke and blubber and long-hung meat.

As May reaches its close there are endless days of crystal clarity when the sun at its height feels hot on his face as if it would burn his skin through. He closes his eyes to its brightness, relishes the heat on his lids, on his temples and cheeks as if it touched the bone beneath. One of these days, a day that is fine as the warmest spring day in England, he does at last a thing he has been thinking to do for weeks. He takes off his clothes in the sun, not only the boots and hat and furs of which he often now divests himself, but jacket and breeches, and linen that is grey and stained and comes off like old fruit peel. The skin he exposes is extraordinarily naked beneath the sunlight, so white that it is almost blued where the shadows fall beneath angular bones, in parts coloured darker where clothing has rubbed and it has been chafed and hardened. He observes his body almost objectively: the pale stomach and ribbed chest, his legs like sticks with a wiry mass of hairs on them, his thin arms hollowed at the elbows, hands at their ends that look huge and black as he turns them before his eyes, the dark tidemarks at his wrists, the other tidemark of filth that he cannot see but can only feel where the skin on his neck beneath his beard is both greasy and engrained with dirt.

He wraps his naked body in a cloak and walks down to a hole in the ice close to the shore. There for the first time he washes, rubbing himself until every part of his body tingles, and it is an extraordinary hard pleasure. He takes up the cloak again and returns to the tent. In his cabin there is other linen, clean linen. But first he throws a broad plank down on the dazzling patch of snow before his door and lies on the smooth wood in the sunshine and basks himself dry.

When he lies on his back he must put a hand across his eyes to shield them from the brightness, to give himself a filtered view that is criss-crossed by the passage of birds overhead. There are so many birds now, moving in gigantic flocks, thousands of birds at a time that come in from the south forming a band in the sky that seems to reach to the very horizon; he sees them approach at first as so many black specks, like particles blown in the smoke from a fire, separating and weaving and drawn together again, hears then the distant uproar of their cries coming closer, long before he can distinguish the individuals, the beat of their wings. He remembers how astonished he had been when he saw the first flock of seabirds, a little flock sudden as an apparition, no more than half a score of birds twittering on a rock on the mountainside. Later that same day a second group arrived, then others in the days that followed, until after a week the mountain and the glacier behind were entirely covered with birds, and they remained two days and then as unexpectedly as they had come they were gone, and he did not know if it was a change in the weather that drove them away or some purpose, some instinct they had that they must move on and breed on some ground even farther north.

Soon as the weather cleared again other flocks came in their wake, eiders and guillemots and other birds he has known at sea, and an innumerable flock of some grey bird the size of a pigeon for which he had no name, and he was as strange to them as they to him, for the birds showed no fear of him or caution and he could almost pluck them out of the sky or off the ground with his hand. He walked among them where they went to nest on the rocks that were now bare of snow, and there were so many of them that they darkened the sky above his head and he could hear nothing beyond their clamour. The little pigeon birds in particular were not much to eat, so little flesh they had on them, but he used their carcases to bait his traps and caught the foxes that were now to be found in numbers surprising for animals of such solitary nature, attracted to the coast he guessed by the presence of the birds.

Now that the winter is over, he has written in his log, *there is such an abundance of creatures and species here that it altogether boggles the mind, such numbers coming off the sea that you had not thought so many creatures could have survived and reproduced themselves since Noah's Flood.*

There were reindeer coming in, coming up to the tent and looking at him without any appearance of fear, and they were lean as sticks after the winter and hardly worth the killing. He did not know from where they had come, and marvelled that they came at all for there was so little for them to feed on at first, the vegetation so recently stripped of snow that it had not even greenness to it yet every patch of pale moss on the mountainside behind the shore was marked with the glossy piles of their droppings.

With such plenty about him he saw that he could choose what he might hunt, knowing that whatever he required for his survival was so infinitesimal that its loss could hardly be reckoned. He phrased a prayer of thanksgiving in his mind and remembered how Adam had lived alongside the beasts in Eden, and made it his rule to kill no more than he needed. Gulls dived so close to his head that their wingtips brushed his hair but he made no attempt to knock them down; their eggs alone were enough to feed five thousand. And then there were the seals that came soon as the ice had broken apart and given them passage, these too in huge herds that played together in the water and then drew themselves on to the beach, steaming and snorting and jostling one another like cattle crowded into a market. The company of the seals touched him as that of none of the other creatures had, some kinship about them that made him at once warm and alone. It was their great uncanny eyes, so redolent of human expression as they popped their heads out from the ice and watched him. They made him conscious of himself as he had not been since he had last seen men, as he had thought he could not be save before another human being.

He walked out on the ice as far as he dared and crouched down on his hunkers before the ice holes and gazed back at them, eye to eye, and at last he began to speak to them, beneath his breath, just for the relief of it, and then one day one of them popped up its head before him and fixed him with such a very human look that he spoke to it aloud. He greeted it and asked it from where it had come, and it turned its head around and looked at him again as if there were indeed words forming there behind its eyes. He laughed at himself then for his fantasy and took himself back to his cabin. Later he went down to the very same hole and this time he had brought his violin with him that he had at last taken down from its pegs on the wall, and he had prepared the bow and tuned its untouched strings as best he could. Seals loved music, the sailors said; there were seals in tales that had human souls and deep under water where men could not see them they danced.

He stood at the edge of the hole in the ice and played, softly, waveringly at first, the notes creaking out of disuse. It was so very long since he had played. So long since he had heard music of any kind. And yet it still existed, he could bring it out of himself. He played to the empty hole and as he did so the tears rose in him and flooded out from his eyes. He held the instrument tighter to his chest then and played the harder, played now from deep within him, played to rouse and exorcise. Suddenly there was a splash and a pop in the hole before him as a seal came up and blew out a spray of water. He played on until his fingers were sore, and took a bow in a second of silence, and not until that was done did the seal dip and disappear.

With the presence of the seals it is as if I live once again in a populated world. Their barks fill the air, and the yelps of the pups that begin to be born now and grow and play at their mothers' sides between the rocks on the strand. The cry of a seal pup is more akin to the cry of a human child than any voice I have otherwise known. Massed together the sound is something like the yells of a mob of children playing, but singly and in distress a man could not I think tell it from the call of fear a human child makes to its parent. I know of no cry so plaintive to my ear as the cry of a seal pup left by its mother alone among the mass. It lies with just the narrow cleft, the idea of a space between itself and all the rest that are strange to it, and reaches up its head and calls that very human and personal cry that seems directed precise as a name, to its mother and to no other. I think that the sense of hearing owned by these beasts must be very acute, for they seem to react to music and even to hear it and be drawn to it from under water, and come then to the surface and crane their necks to listen.

15

THOMAS CAVE WALKS among the seals and either they are not aware of his presence or they trust the man as if he were one of their own. The colony is incessantly watchful, ever a number of heads raised to look about for a source of danger, those at the edge ready at the slightest notice to plunge back off rock or ice into the sea. The sight of a bear runs through the massed bodies like an earthquake and scatters hundreds at an instant's delay. Yet, Thomas Cave observes, the seals have not learnt yet what he knows: the danger inherent in a man.

Does not one of them remember last summer, how the men of the *Heartsease* came amongst them and clubbed hundreds of their number in a single working shift? How on days when the ice drove in or the bay was held in fog the whalers kept on shore and walked through the strands of mist between the blackness of rock and the blur of snow, weaved among the dense herds of parents and young and clubbed them, one after another? The seals were such easy hunting, so easy to stun them with a single blow of the club to the nose and then to finish them with a knife, hunting as easy and as close as killing a pig in a yard. They butchered them where they killed them and stripped them of their blubber, tens, hundreds at a time, and boiled all the blubber down into oil so that the fishery was thick with the grease and smoke of industry even when they had no sight of a whale.

It seems fantastical to recall, such slaughter in this one spot. The butchery, the boiling, that went on here, the scavenging gulls and the stink of carcases. Yet even now on those rare and lovely days when the sun warms the residues in the boilers and on the ground, a whiff of it trails again in the air.

Where the snow becomes soft and waterlogged, a red staining appears and begins to spread across it. This I have observed in past years, when we have come in the summer and found sometimes whole fields of snow that are stained pinkish red right across their surface. I have met no man yet who could explain to me what it is that causes this curious discoloration.

He cannot understand and yet, this year of all years, the phenomenon seems to him to signify a meaning.

Carnock's big laugh, that echoed off the hardness of rock.

'I'll give you a show, boys.'

Mister Carnock, Mate of the *Heartsease*, pulling in his

audience like a man with a freak to show at a fair. He had never liked Carnock, had taken him from the first as a loud, bragging man, knew him the more so as he swaggered in the bows of the whaleboat as it passed beneath the cliff.

A small herd of seals, stragglers that had had their pups late, on the rocks of the point, only a few of them, slipping into the sea as the boat approached. There was one pup that was very pale and marked with white, just three foot long, and it was cornered in a shallow pool among the rocks, no room for it to dive beneath the boat and join the others that seemed to wait out in the open sea. Carnock threw a net about it and caught it alive, unharmed.

'There's a beauty!' He pulled it in, held it upside down like a trophy, held it by its tail so that its head thrashed against the sides of the boat. Carnock was not a tall man but strong. You could see the strength in his shoulders, even in the way he stood, braced and square.

He threw the pup down on to the floor of the boat and called for men to hold it still. One man sat astride it. Another held its head. Its eyes were huge, rolling, white-edged.

Carnock was precise with his knife, slitting first behind the ears and then along its stomach and around the tail. Every man present had seen a seal flayed before, many times, but never one alive, nor ever heard such yelps of pain. The boat rocked as it writhed about in the pool of blood and bilge.

'There's my baby, there it goes!'

The three of them eventually succeeded in heaving it over the side and back into the sea. It was so slippery without its skin that they had dropped it many times. In the water it straightened and shot off to join the rest, its strength apparently undiminished, and the other seals came and swam about it in a frenzy, frisking and barking in such a strange way that, were it not for the reddening of the water, it might have seemed a celebration.

Thomas Cave heard the laughter of the men about him. It was mob laughter and he closed his ears to it. Inside him was only a terrible silence. His awareness was all for the seal, a mangled length of muscle that continued to swim away with a wake of blood behind it, one long swimming wound like a gash in the sea itself.

As the bay clears of ice it becomes his habit to climb to his lookout on the mountain to watch for the ship as he used to for the sun. Some moments he thinks he cannot bear his isolation a day more, and his longing turns ice floes into sails and makes ships where they do not exist; and yet it can seem a reprieve when a storm comes and holds him again tight indoors as he was through the winter, and when he emerges to see that the ice has come back in. Even as he yearns for the company of men he dreads their return.

Blotches of red on the snow below. A cry that rises to him, the cry of a seal or walrus cub. It is like the cry of a human child.

He remembers how it came at last. The birth. The midwife calling to him, and he going in. The slippery being in her hands, a blind limp thing mouthing for breath like a bloodied fish in air. Its mother dying beside it, the blood run out of her.

THE NARRATIVE
OF THOMAS GOODLARD
Related on the Suffolk coast, two summer evenings of 1640

At Duke's Cove

16

THAT VOYAGE BACK was slow, slow as if the *Heart-sease* herself were reluctant to go north. I remember that I ached with the slowness of it. I was so young, eager with youth. I was at that age when any time of tedium seemed like a weight that dragged against me.

The winds were fickle from the outset, a chill head wind blowing up all of a sudden as we lifted anchor at Hull on a pretty May morning though we had seen another ship slip away ahead of us on the very same tide. Two days then we were held before the mouth of the Humber, riding out the nights first at Paull Road and then at Clee Ness, looking out from the stubborn river across land that was glum even under the brightness of spring, of such dreary flatness that not even the rise of a great church spire across the marshes could make it friendly to the eye.

Slow we came out to sea, slow round the mean tongue of earth that bent across the river mouth, and the waves when we met them were welcome, iron grey after the mud-stained water of the river. Yet even as the sails filled I felt a heaviness in me like that of the dullest calm, and wondered if the others on the ship felt it also. I cannot say if this was so. Perhaps to them it was like any, another voyage, nothing particular to it, only life passing. Perhaps I alone was so aware because I kept that money still, his coins held for all of that year in my trunk as in a hot fist.

We were the same men who had gone before, most of us. There was Carnock; there was the same band of a dozen Biscayans who had gone on south to their own people for the winter but returned now to Hull and to Marmaduke, a face or two among them changed but the same dark and wiry look to all and the same aloofness from the rest; and there were others too, sailors, carpenters, coopers, that I knew from before. Captain Duke had brought his son with him, his first time out, a lad little more than myself in age but with a cocksure manner and a burn to his look that made me shy of him. Edward Marmaduke stood beside his father on the deck, the image of him only fleshier, without the elder man's compactness, and despite, or perhaps it was because of, his youth and inexperience seemed to look down at us and out to the flat line of the horizon as if he had nothing but certainty of what lay beyond it.

North we went, along the coast past the high cliff church of Whitby, close in past the great Bass Rock that flickered white with gulls, along the dour coast of Scotland and across the open sea to Shetland, where again we added a last couple of men to the crew. I have made that route so many times I have each landmark of it imprinted on my memory but never I think was I so aware of each stage of the passage as on that second fretful voyage. My eye at once clung to each successive piece of land and at the same moment wanted it gone behind me, wanted the journey done. There was both dread and longing in the idea of the ice and the northern seas, of the cold and the fog and the dazzle, the stark impossibility of a landscape whose forms are like the peaks and troughs of waves but moulded hard out of rock and ice. Even when you have once visited the North it seems when you have been away from it scarcely believable, its unearthly atmospheres a dream and delusion of the senses. Less probable still is the idea of a lone man's survival in such a place.

We did not speak of him, the man I remembered. Yet whenever I looked up ahead of us, when a cloud turned the sea to lead or when the sun came out and made it shine like silver, I held his figure small in the back of my mind like a mark that I could not erase. Again I say that I do not know how it was with the others but I know that he was with me through the day and in the cramped darkness of the night. I believed that he was Captain Duke's preoccupation also, for never had I seen the Captain so impatient as on this voyage. From the dock outwards, even from the moment of our loading, he had tramped about the deck chivvying and swearing, chafing at each little delay, that small, powerful, dark man stomping and blowing so that I thought of a small black bull in a pen. Those who knew him best said that it was not like him to be so tight. He did not even let us halt, as was the usual pattern, to do some sealing on the way, though we sighted great numbers of seals in the clear weather as we left the Shetlands. No, he must hurry us on. A southerly breeze was a direct gift from God to the *Heartsease* and it would be sin to turn across it, but we must put our sails full before it; and even if it dropped, as ever and again on that trip it did, falling away soon as we had it behind us, we would set our course that way and no other. There was the inevitable grumbling among the men at that, mutterings that made the mood on board at times difficult and sullen, but none spoke loud against it. It was clear I think to others besides myself that Marmaduke's frustration was born of this particular cause, that he was driven so not by the requirements of the whaling but by the simple need to see whether or not his man had perished.

When we got there, the great fjord was still blocked by ice. We knew of the ice before we reached it, for the lookout at the masthead had a day before seen the reflection of it on the clouds up ahead. To those with experience of the North, it shows like that, a frozen sea: a white glare on the underbelly of the clouds as if they are lit by a harsh light beneath them.

But for Cave we might have turned straight about and worked along the western coasts which we knew were free. We had seen whales already on the sea, heard them blow and seen their distant spouts; there was every hope of a good season. Instead we sailed slowly about the edge of this ice, teasing at every apparent opening, looking for a passage, hoping to see it slacken. After two days we met a pair of whaleships out of Amsterdam, and they were coming to us from the direction in which we were headed. Not a chance, they said, the westerly winds were only packing the ice more densely with each day that passed. They were going south to Jan Mayen. There was consolation, they said, in the knowledge that if the ice held us back then it must also hold back the whales. Captain Duke put that down to the complacency of their nation and sailed restlessly on, went up to the masthead himself and spent stubborn freezing hours there wrapped in canvas, looking for a break in the frozen ocean or any sign of it in the sky. These were eerie days, endless days for it was by then the end of June and we were far north. Often there was fog, a fine fog with crystals of ice in it that you felt in your nose when you breathed, and visibility was close and we could do nothing but wait. And then the sky would clear and we could see for a great distance, and the sun showed above the horizon for all of the twenty-four hours and threw strange colours and long shadows across the ruckled surface of the ice. At times the creeping shadow of the *Heartsease* extended for miles, her black bulk, her three masts, even the figures on her deck, and yet never had I felt the ship to be so small and insignificant, puny as a beetle fidgeting along the edge of that frozen sheet of space. Even though I was young I had an extreme sense of man's smallness and the futility of all his works. That is what it does to you, a place like that.

The storm when it came was almost welcome. Storms come fast up there, the weather like the passage of the hours so much more intense than it is in our moderate land. There was barely time to put off what seemed a safe distance from the ice edge to ride it out. Only a day, but it was like a day of most savage winter, wind and snow like knives and a mountainous black sea. The *Heartsease* was broad and sturdy like the Ark and we prayed that the Lord would preserve us and huddled within its heaving timbers and felt and listened to the storm. And through it, beneath the howl of the wind and the crash of the water, we thought we heard a thunder that was the ice cracking, and when we came again on deck must watch in terror as pieces of it came hurtling at us in the waves.

Morning came and the air was still though the ship continued to toss with the power of the storm. I had slept some hours at last and I woke and came on deck, and it was as if a conjuring trick had been performed there and opened the fjord before us. The solid icescape that we had known so well for all those days, every bay and peninsula and hummock of it, was gone, and in its place was a dark blue sea with a great swell on it, and great blocks of ice drifting past us, clean-broken ice with glassy tints of turquoise and green to it in the light. We said a prayer and began a slow passage north to the place we called Duke's Cove – it still has that name even now, though sometimes changed by the Hollanders' use to Dusko or Disko. Our progress was slow because the sea was still big and the broken ice was a danger to us, some of it floating almost submerged and showing only in a ghostly manner beneath the surface of the water so that lookouts had to be constantly posted to watch against any collision that might cause damage to the hull.

Again we heard whales, and saw them break the water but too far off still for the hunting. Sometimes we could see right across the fjord, some thirty miles or more, to the savage dark walls and peaks on either side, their black and purplish rock bared since the storm though snow held to the ravines and valleys and on the glaciers, and then a fog would roll out down the channel and the world would suddenly contract to the familiar one of wood and canvas and Englishmen and water, and I would feel that I had seen a vision that had never existed. A fog like that came upon us just as we approached the bay where we had left Cave, and Captain Duke would not risk the ship in close but asked for volunteers to take one of the boats in and look if he was alive.

I was one of those who stepped forward, and a half-dozen others who included Ezkarra the Biscayan harpooneer, and Marmaduke's son Edward, though his father forbade it at first and said he should wait and land with the rest when the time came; but Edward pressed him, he was ever one to get his way, until his father agreed that there was no danger but only adventure to the outing. The last man to step out to join the boat, even as it was lowered into the sea, was Carnock, and it seemed right that he was there.

We rowed slowly through strands of fog, the oars some-times slapping against plates of ice, the water strange and greenish when there was light upon it, the ice dark and discoloured. The land when we saw it loomed high above our heads, the cliffs and rocks seeming so tall and unfamiliar that for some moments I did wonder whether we were in fact in the right place or whether we had overshot the point and come to some other unknown bay further up the coast. 'That's it, over there. We'll pull up on the shore there.' Carnock knew it. He had been there many more seasons than I. It was a rare kindness in him to take the time to explain to me that the apparent height of the land was an illusory effect of the fog.

Perhaps we all felt that there was time to spare, going ashore at last in that grey and melancholy silence, time to spare and to lose. As the hull of the boat grounded the man in its bow cleared the lip of the waves with a great soft leap and pulled us in. We came behind him slow, one after the other. The fog let through a muted light and all the ground beyond where the sea had washed was a floury white, powdered over with a fine new snow.

'Which way is it?'

Whoever spoke did no more than whisper, but the question carried through our huddle.

'Here, to the right. See, we have landed somewhat down the shore from our accustomed place.' Carnock of all of us seemed to know best where he was, and his square form led the way then along and up the beach.

We followed in a loose line like a knotted string, walking with unsteady steps as we had so soon come to land, taking bearings, stumbling on the shingle and over rocks that were capped with snow. Marmaduke's son walked just before me, then stopped and held a moment until I came alongside that he might speak what he was pressing to say.

'What a place! I had not imagined it could be so dismal as this.'

'It's dismal now but wait till you see it when it clears.'

'So cold, the fog so thick that it clogs the eyes. It is like a place of doom.'

'Wait,' I said. 'Wait until you see it on a day of sun. It's beautiful then, all crystal and dazzling.'

He looked away as if he did not believe me, walked on, then stopped and turned his head again.

'And you were here last year, and you knew this man Cave?'

'That was the first time I came.'

'Was he not afraid, to do what he did? Why, I would not be alone here a single day!'

So brightly he said it that the men must have heard all up and down our line. (Looking back, knowing what was to come later, I wonder now if it was not some premonition in him that heightened his first impression of the place.)

Whoever heard, none answered him. No more words there were for some time, but only a muttered curse as a man tripped, the tread of our boots and the pulse of the sea that was behind us and already lost in fog. The cookery loomed up slowly. Hard to know it at first, coming at it from that unfamiliar angle, it was all so still and shrouded and quiet.

'There! Over there! Is that it?'

Edward spoke full out and the sudden freshness of his voice shook me like a shout in church. Did he have no fear, no respect? Or was his excitement driven by his fear?

There was no sign of living man to be seen. Nothing disturbed, no footprint besides our own, no marks on the snow save the spider tracks of birds. The tent stood before us like a great square tomb.

And then we heard a sound which my ear at first took for wind, some strange effect of wind despite the stillness about us; so sure was my fatalism that this was what I thought before my consciousness recognised the sound for what I knew of course it was: the sound of a violin.

Ezkarra pulled out the cross he wore about his neck and kissed it, speaking a gravelly prayer beneath his breath.

161

'See, boy, so your friend lives after all.'

He held the cross to me that I too might kiss it. It was a plain, savage-looking cross that he had made himself from whalebone and engraved with a long and contorted Christ. I had a sudden urge to make the gesture, alien though it was to me.

And then Carnock spoke darkly and made us all afraid. 'Unless it be his ghost.'

No ghost he was but changed. How changed I was to learn only in time. To me then, seeing him, all the change I saw was physical: how thin he was, how his hands dangled off him, how old he looked, and how still his eyes.

He did not see us as we entered. His back was turned, his head bent, his body swaying with the tune which seemed some sedate lament. It was extraordinary for being so homely, the sight of a man playing his music by lamplight in a warm room, a fire in the stove, a scrubbed table holding the remnants of a meal, a high cot covered in furs, a pretty embroidered cloth hung on the wall. When he saw us, or rather, felt our presence, for he did not turn immediately, he lowered the fiddle and spoke without any tone of surprise.

'Ah, so there you are.'

He might have said the same if we had been gone only a week or a morning.

'What kept you? I had been expecting you.'

He looked a decade, not a winter, older. He looked older than my father whom I had seen so little a time before as

Easter. There was more sense of age in him in that moment than in any old man I ever knew. He was old like an apostle or a prophet carved at the door of a church. His hair and beard were long and matted, the lines on his face deep and etched with soot, his hands that held the instrument thin and knobbled, the whole of him thin. Thomas Cave had been gaunt already but now he was a man of sticks; his head and hands, the feet that weighed him down, all seemed too heavy for the frame that held them.

He moved those long limbs with a strange gentleness, as if they were very fragile, or as if he were a saint from a statue only that moment come to life. He looked at us without surprise or shock of recognition, laid the fiddle gently across the scrubbed table and the bow beside it. I noticed how clean the table was, how neatly the cabin was arranged, and wondered if he had cleaned it in expectation of our arrival. Only the roof space above our heads had not been swept: the rafters and the chimney hood were coated with great black flakes of soot, and as we stood there the draught that came through the open door set them fluttering down like leaves from trees in the forest and showered the table and the floor. With a skeletal hand Thomas Cave flicked at one that clung to the mat of hair on his brow, and for the first time now an expression crossed his face. I think that it was a smile.

17

H E WOULD NOT come to sleep on board the ship with us that night but insisted that he remain in his cabin. That seemed lonely to us but we could see how it was his home. He had offered us his best hospitality, a cup of water which we must pass around and a plate of some strong black stew of venison. We had taken a small portion out of politeness though in truth it was pretty vile. When we left him we said that we would be back the next day with ale and wine and whatever else he asked for, and that we would take him then to visit the ship.

As we slept the wind changed and cleared the fog and the tide swept the last of the ice away from the shore. The day to which we woke was as unlike the one before it as any two days can be: bright in that way that is peculiar to the North and that I have seen nowhere else, bright with that rare, sharp, glassy light, and we took the *Heartsease* in a little way and dropped anchor as close as we might to the shore. Thomas Cave did not say a word as we rowed him out, but gazed on her and looked all about him rather as a child does in a new place.

'Is this the same ship on which I came?' he asked at last. 'She looks so big.'

She looked the bigger the closer we got, her sturdy hull rising above us in the water. The receding cold had left every surface of her coated with a thick rime, her decks, her furled sails, her rigging all glistening with slivers of frost, and the air about her glistened with crystals that fell away with each moment in the sunlight.

'Why, she is like an island.'

He climbed up on deck and Marmaduke greeted him closely and hugged him, and then took him away to his cabin. He had with him the book in which he had recorded all the details of his survival, a logbook wrapped around with cloth that he had held tight to his chest all the time that we rowed him out to the ship. I do not know what was in it, though at that time I longed to. I longed for stories, for the tale of his adventure that he was never in my hearing to divulge. I reckon that that book he gave to the Captain had in it all that he was ever to say of his experience.

'See how he clutched the book to him. There is madness in it.'

Marmaduke did not come out for hours and we worked without him, to and fro from ship to beach, bringing on to land our stores and all the cumbersome equipment of our summer's business. It is like setting up a little town, putting together a whaling station, all the barrels and tools as well as the hoists and coppers and furnaces.

'Did you see the way he looked at the ship? He may have survived but he's lost a part of his mind. Something's frozen in him.'

'When we came upon him, that first moment when he saw us, I had a feeling that he did not like it. I thought that he did not want to see us at all.'

'Of course he did, wouldn't any man? How could you doubt it?'

Again we rowed back empty to the ship through water that was so clear that we could see the shadow of our boat on the sand beneath. Each one of us had been watching Cave and puzzling over him.

'I know what you mean,' said another. 'It makes no sense, but it was how he looked when we came in. The blank way he looked at us.'

'He's just a trifle mad. Who wouldn't be in the circumstances?'

'He was mad from the start if you ask me, mad to say he'd do such a thing.'

'Cave is not mad but dazzled.' Joseph Hailey had more knowledge of the northern seas than any of us save Marmaduke, had sailed up there a decade or more. 'I have seen that look in men's eyes before. Once I went with a Danish ship to the west of Greenland, and there is a tribe of men who live there, dark sturdy hunters who know the ways of living amongst the ice. I saw the same in them, in men we met alone when we put in along the coast, men who must have been away from their people for many days. I imagine that it is like a kind of snow dazzle, when you look before you but see only whiteness. They say that sometimes in those parts it comes upon a man so bad that he runs away from everyone he meets, away into the white, and is never seen again.'

Mad, dazzled, yet the proof of his sanity was there in material things before our eyes: the order of his cabin which demonstrated the orderliness of his life through the months of his hermitage, the cooking arrangements, the cobbling tools and the ranks of wooden heels he had made that were enough to fill a whole barrel when at last we went home. Then there was his apparent physical health, despite his thinness, and all the evidence of his hunting: the great bearskin that he had scraped and spread on poles to cure, one bigger than any I had ever seen, its thick fur almost butter-coloured in that day's bright and melting light, and the many bones and carcases of other animals that were strewn about, both close by the tent and further off where he had butchered them at the site of his kill.

I wonder now if the madness that we thought we saw in him that day was in part a reflection of the fear in ourselves? We looked at him and did not see Thomas Cave but imagined only the cold and the darkness and the solitude, and did not think that we could bear it, and I could not have said which one of these three horrors to me was the worst.

It would have made it easier for us if he had told us tales. Words, our English words, would have reduced all that we imagined to reality, put the miracle of his survival into pieces that we could hold. But he chose not to speak, or perhaps he could not find the words to speak with. Only physical information escaped him. He told us of his discovery that the place where we were, which we had supposed to be an extension to the east of the land that we already knew as Greenland, was not so but an island on its own, and he pointed out where on a clear day we might climb to ascertain this fact. He told us where particular herbs and grasses might be found among the mosses and the lichens on the mountainsides. He had learned better than the most experienced of the sailors the ways of the northern weather, could predict its moods and sudden changes. Yet all this he told us in connection with the present time only, and never did he refer back to what was past. All that was left for us to guess and wonder at.

'You ask him, Goodlard, he'll talk to you,' the others said to me. 'Why, last year we saw that you were like a son to him.'

I tried, believe me. My curiosity was as great as anyone's. But Cave seemed not to hear us, and looked across to us from that distance of his and held his silence. Even now, and I was his companion for some long time after that voyage was done and we had returned to England, I have nothing to tell you of what occurred to him in that winter. I cannot even say what injury it was that caused the slight limp which I discerned in him, which he was never to lose, some injury which he must have sustained to the ankle or the knee of his right leg that just so little skewed his walk. I thought it like the limp that Jacob had after he had wrestled with God in his dream and God had struck him. The mark of God on him, that's what I thought it was.

18

THE WAY I talk now, it seems as if Thomas Cave was at the centre of my thoughts all of that summer. This was not so, of course. I recount only what my memory selects and what it seems of interest to tell, the things that stand out and are particular to that one season of the many I have spent up there in the Greenland seas. The truth of it is that I did not much preoccupy myself with Cave, not after those first few days of finding him again. How could I when there was so much else, so much that was more immediate and demanding of the senses?

I do not know if you have seen a whale. It is a beast of a size which it is only reasonable to imagine in the vastness of the ocean. On land it seems monstrous and alien. Did you hear the story how, only a couple of years ago, one came up the river close by Ipswich? It was washed there by some freak, and men heard of it and crowded to the estuary, and came out in boats and on to the mud when the tide was down with every kind of weapon they could muster, spears, swords, guns, hatchets, billhooks and axes, and tried to kill it as it floundered in what little water remained for it to swim in. They did not succeed in making a death blow until they had an anchor stuck in its nostril and it was gushing blood, like water from a pump, and all those about the river were red as if they had worked in a slaughterhouse; and then they cut it up into thousands of pieces, that any man or woman or child that had tuppence to pay for it might take home, and some ate their meat while others put it away like some famous relic and accounted it a wonder and a marvel. And before they cut up the whale a man had the wit to measure it, and it was a full fifty-eight foot in length, twelve foot high, and two foot between the eyes.

Take that to your mind and then imagine the whales as they are in their own element, in the sea, whales of this size and more, swimming north up the broad sea of the great fjord. We could see them from the rocks of the point, see the tracks they made in the water, the spouts they blew like so many fountains shooting into the air, see their black backs as they surfaced and their great shining tails which they thrashed into the sea with a sound like a whipcrack that carried for miles. They came in flocks, scores of them as you would commonly see shoals of fish, more spouts and tails than you could begin to count, and many of them came into the calm of the bay as if they would bask and play there all the summer, only that the *Heartsease* was there waiting for them.

The first whale was killed within two days of our coming, killed at the mouth of the bay and three boats towed it back to the ship, floating belly-up and trailing red clouds in the water, a huge old beast whose crinkled skin was all barnacled and thick with sea lice, and it was tied up there to the stern of the ship, still floating, and we left it a day to settle before we began the task of butchery.

This butchery is work on a scale that you cannot imagine if you have slaughtered only pigs or cattle, work that is more like the activity of ants when they combine to pull away to their nest some great cockroach or scrap of dead meat twenty times their size: the dismantling and transferral on to shore of the pieces of a beast that may be almost as long as a ship itself, a piece of prey and yet it towers above the men who work on it, who walk on it and slip on its skin, who cut at it with great knives that seem proportionately no more than pins. The blubber lies directly beneath the hard black skin, a broad layer of yellowish lard. Slice at it sharp and sidelong as a butcher slices the fat off a piece of meat, and it pulls away clean, clean in itself too at first as if you might eat it, buttery coloured and pure and smelling of nothing but itself, though if it is left under a warm sun it soon becomes putrid and sets off a stink that clings like its grease to all that touches it.

There's a skill to this that we call flensing, like the skill of a master butcher, and it was one of the Biscayans who did that work, a little dark bow-legged man who walked barefoot on the whale and never lost his grip. Cave, always neat with his hands, used to work with him; I saw that sometimes, saw the two of them, tall and small, progressing down the body of the beast where it lay in the water, cutting blocks and stripping them off, long slabs of blubber like tombstones oozing oil. Sometimes Cave was not there and the Biscayan worked alone or took some other one of us to help in Cave's stead. The pieces of blubber they threw down to the sea to be towed ashore, and there we chopped them down further, raked them up and ladled them into a great tub that hung from the arm of a gibbet that turned to and fro between the chopping benches and the coppers upon the furnaces. Picture this if you can in such a scene of cold grandeur as only those northern coasts can produce: the smallness of the men and the ugliness of their contrivances, the smoke, the soot, the pervasive oil and its ever more pungent smell, and above it all the voracious flocks of birds that at every stage attended us, the gulls swirling and diving amongst us.

And then there is the reverse of the process: the removal of the rendered blubber; its steam and sizzle as it is ladled into cooling vats filled with water; how it is drained out and down a series of gutters and coolers and at last into the barrels. Meantime others have cut off the head from the beast and brought it in and drawn it up on the shore as far as they and the tide can pull it, for it is heavy with bone, and walked in between its jaws and sliced out all the slim fins of whalebone and scraped them down and rubbed them with sand. Besides what meat we choose to cut – and the meat is good, red and fleshy like the richest beef and not at all like fish or anything that comes out of the sea – the rest of the whale is waste, and is left to sink or wash to and fro in the water of the bay which close to the shore has become dense and still, so loaded it is with grease.

That summer the work like the days never seemed to end. We took fifteen whales, near one thousand five hundred hogsheads of oil, barrel upon barrel floated out again and loaded on to the ship. It was a great catch. And the weather was free of storms and, until the end, free of that stifling fog, day after day of workable if chill weather with most times a layer of cloud to take the sharpness from the sky and keep our shadow off the sea to make the fishing good. All in all it would have seemed an exceptional and lucky season despite the slowness of its start, a blessed season even, were it not for those things that happened at its close.

Until those events there is nothing much that I can tell you of Cave. I can give you only these odd pictures of him that I keep in my mind: walking among us on shore like a shadow, hair and beard trimmed, his strangeness muted as he assimilated once more into the company of others; or grimly working the carcase of a whale where it floated at the stern of the ship, atop the black and shining mound, his gaunt figure with the flensing knife in its hand silhouetted one day like a stag oak against a rare bright sky. I remember that I came beneath him in a boat as we tied the whale in and he spoke and gestured, but in that light he could see me so much more clearly than I might see him, and there was only his outline rearing down on me and his expression was indeciperable.

A fine day, I think I called that it was a fine day, and indeed the sun fell hot on my face and dazzled as I looked up to him.

I was not sure of the words I caught coming down. The pity of it, it might have been, but I hear him now with twenty years of hindsight. Could it have been that? That is how I picture it now. There is the sea, the ship, the carcase of the whale, all raw with the brightness of the day, and Thomas Cave stretches out his arms in an awkward frame about the scene, and that is what he says.

Some days I saw that he worked and then for some days he was not there. I heard it mentioned that there was a madness on him, but others said that it was not so much a madness as a melancholy, that he had gone to sit alone in some dark corner like a brooding hen. And when he was in the company of men it was the Biscayans he sought rather than ourselves. The Biscayans were a haughty and separate bunch and I never saw any other Englishmen find any level of intimacy with them, even those who had picked up a piece of their language or spoke some French or Spanish or whatever tongue it was that they had in common. Yet they took to Cave and sometimes when work was done I saw that he sat and ate and drank with them.

The other pictures I have of him are from that summer's end, the weather already on the turn and the nights beginning and the looking-out for ice.

I see Cave standing for hours on end on the rocks of the point on the northern tip of the bay when all the sea before him is swathed in fog, standing alert, listening where he could not see, as if with his ears he might penetrate where his eyes are blind.

Carnock's boat was lost. Six men in it, counting himself. It was last seen by one of the other whaleboat crews as the fog was rolling in, no more than a hundred, a hundred and fifty yards' visibility, they said, and it was chasing a whale. The boats behind had heard the yell of the harpooner as he made contact, the surge and the zip of the rope as the whale pulled away, and followed though they could not see in what direction it was gone. And that was the end of it. Not a sound, not a cry more, they said, no sight, but only the strip of frothing water that they came to where they knew the whale had fought.

No way could they tell what had occurred. A chase like that is terrifying in the fog. The whale pulls away and the men on the harpoon boat that holds to it cannot know where they go nor reckon how far, nor how close the other boats remain behind them or if they will be able to follow and pick them up should they be overturned into the sea. I have heard of boats dragged many miles blind in that way and scarcely able to find their way home, and of others more fearful who swiftly cut the rope that tied them to the whale. Carnock was not the sort of man to have taken that course, we knew that Carnock would have held on long as he could. How far the whale took him and his men we could not begin to guess. It could have been hours, days, out into the fjord and the ocean beyond; or it was possible that it was a few minutes only, a mere snatch of time, and that they were pulled down into the vortex of the whale's dive or simply overturned by a flick of its tail and drowned close by us unseen and unheard in the muffling confusion of the fog.

I was at the cookery when the news of it came to me, in the heat of boiling blubber. A boat lost out in the bay, and I took in the words and worked on as I must for the fire was up and needed stoking. I did not even know till after who was in it, not until I wiped the grease off me and went to the water's edge.

Some few of us were left there on the shore. Most had

gone out in the boats and we could hear their calls though we could not see them.

It was a time before we put together the names of all that were there with Carnock: a harpooneer that was one of two Biscayan brothers, a sailor called Jonas Watson who had been good to me, two others that I knew not well, and Edward Marmaduke. That shocked me, to hear that. All of it was a shock, even though it was an occurrence that is ever, in those seas, half-awaited, such things are always a shock when they become fact. Yet this loss, this sneaking fog-bound silent loss, touched us more than any for the loss of the Captain's son, and the Captain loved by all and the son no more than my age and such a vivid strutting cockerel of a boy.

The boats stayed out for hours, far longer than any swimmer might have lasted in that cold and inky water, zigzagging across the empty sea, calling out and staring into nothingness. We on the land walked the shore along the full length of the bay, looking and calling likewise, drawn to every other looming rock to see if it might be a piece of boat or a man washed up.

I came upon Cave at the rocky point on the northern spur of the bay. It was a good place to stand as the current swept by there. I went and stood beside him and he lifted a hand to me and would not speak but only listen, his concentration so intense that I felt it myself, and felt as I stood there beside him that I could hear more closely the movement of the waves, make out in it any slight erratic distant sound that might have been that of an oar.

Once I heard a call that I thought could be that of a man.

'Only a seal,' he whispered. 'Listen, it is more like the cry of a child than of a man.'

Just then a flight of gulls passed overhead and the sound was lost but I believed that what he said was true.

At last even he gave up his watch, and it was he who went out to Captain Marmaduke, who had waited shut in his cabin all of this time, and later the two of them came back to shore and walked in the half-light.

I think that for a grown man it is like his own death to lose his only son; a double death, for a man means his son to follow on, to carry on his name and be his escape from his own mortality. Captain Marmaduke took it hard. He walked a long time with Cave and then he had them row him back to the ship, and went straight to his cabin and did not come out of it for days on end. By that time it was late in August. The whales were on the move away and we too began to pack up on shore, loaded the hold, waited for the word to sail. The fog that had swallowed the boat persisted about us, sometimes thinning, sometimes giving way to flakes of snow. These were days of mourning and of awful tension. We prayed the prayers for the drowned but looked at the water and all of us I believe still hoped to see a form emerge from it or hear the creak of the returning boat within the mist, and at the same time we looked at the ship where the Captain was closed away and longed to be gone.

19

MANY OF US in that time found that we could not
sleep, so much the rhythm of night and day had
been broken in us. In the tent where we stayed together
there was scarcely a moment of stillness for all the
turning and sighs of waking men. Even those who did
sleep were not at peace. We all of us had strange and
heavy dreams, and often men muttered in their sleep or
moaned or sometimes woke themselves and the rest of us
with a yell.

So it was that fear began to grow in us.

When we slept, there were the dreams. When we
woke, there was something else I cannot name. I remember lying there and feeling the hugeness of the place
thud in my soul where the knowledge of God had been, a
huge frozen emptiness inside and a fear that it would
expand and consume me. I shared a bunk with William
Sherwyn, a restless knotty little man all knees and elbows.
When I opened my eyes I saw that he lay on his back

staring upward, and he became aware of me and spoke in a nervous rush. 'You know what it is, don't you? You know what this means? The ice will come in soon. The currents drive it early up the fjord, that's why no one but Captain Duke will bring a ship in here. Someone said that to me, back in Hull before we sailed. You chance your luck with Duke, he said, he's a great whaler of course and he knows those northern seas better than any other Englishman but one of these days he'll be caught, beset, held fast, and that'll be the end of it. It happens to all the great navigators, he said. It happened to Barents. It'll happen to him. They all go too far in the end, stay too long. Sail too close to the ice.'

'It's August,' I said, 'only August.'

'We were gone by this day last year.'

'Last year was colder.'

'Doesn't take long for the ice to come in. All it takes is a change of wind.'

'But it's only a day's sail out to the cape and the sea.' I shut my eyes again and imagined the movement of the ship as it would be beneath me, the sight of the southernmost cape of those islands receding, the knowledge of open water down to the coast of Norway. I must then have slept a little. When I was next conscious Sherwyn was holding me.

'What is it, lad? What is it makes you scream?'

Only a piece of my dream stayed in my head: the terrible sensation of falling into utter and endless icy space.

If only the fog had lifted. If there had been light to see by: God's light, God's day. We would have seen the crispness of the sea where the lost boat had been and known for sure that no one was to come back from it. Captain Duke would have seen it also. He would have come to the deck and called us to weigh anchor. But the fog held us there suspended, its muffled forms and sounds offering so many possibilities of denial. It was the sounds most of all: the bark of a walrus that one of us took for a man's call; the way the screech of gulls would erupt all of a sudden out of intense silence; the creak of footfalls on snow; the lapping of water against the rocks which was at moments like the plash of oars. Sometimes it seemed that we waited for men, sometimes for ghosts. There was a murmur went about that the place had bewitched us and would not let us go.

There is power in the Biscay language. I know nothing of it, only that it is different from any others I hear, the people of that region a race distinct though they have no land but only a sea to call their own, and that the roughest sea in Europe. Their speech is full of harsh zeds and k's, savage sounds and angry rhythms that make our English by comparison seem soft and sleepy. Screamed out in a close room it claws and tears at the nerves like no other sound I have ever heard.

It was the flenser, the little bow-legged man who cut the whale. He was out of his bunk in the centre of the cramped room, half-dressed and screaming at us all wild-eyed. I thought something had happened, that there was a landslide or a bear at the door, or that he had been out and seen that the ship had gone and left us. Or that there was some quarrel between him and one of the others of his people, for the rest of them either got down or sat up in their bunks and set to yelling back. It was truly a scene from Bedlam, this incomprehensible ranting to and fro, and the dazed looks of the rest of us as we stirred in its midst.

I do not know how many of you have seen a man gone mad. You do not want to look, and yet you do, and when you do he draws you into his horror. All of us watched as Ezkarra, the tall harpooneer who was often the leader among them, made the others hush and went and took the little man tight in his arms as if he were a child. For an instant he was silenced, and dropped the lids on his staring eyes, and I thought that he was soothed, but it was only an instant like the trough of a wave and then his mouth frothed again and he broke out and struck Ezkarra so hard in the stomach that it doubled him over, and launched again into such a grotesque stream of words that I knew that they could be nothing but blasphemies and obscenities.

We stood back then, made a way for him as he ran to the door, backing away from him in the cramped space as if from some contamination. He is possessed, we said, and it was shocking to think that a devil had come and possessed one amongst us and left the rest of us sane. Ezkarra then called us to silence and spoke to us in his English. The man was the brother of the harpooneer from the lost boat, he told us. He had the spirit of his drowned brother in him. And he crossed himself and said a popish prayer. Yet others of the crew whispered as instantly that it was some witch amongst us or some demon of the place who possessed him, that this man was only the first and that his madness would come to all of us in time. For myself, I did not speculate but could only watch and follow. I put on my jacket and boots and followed where the man had gone. Some others did likewise. We went out and kept a watch on him as he threw himself down on the stones before the shore and rolled over and over and beat his head against them.

He beat himself bloody and then Ezkarra went again to soothe him, and again he would not be soothed, but this time he ran and took up his flensing knife where it lay among the tools and came back at Ezkarra as if he would slice him in two. I cannot say why it was that he did not, but stalled with the long-handled knife in the air like a maddened, half-naked Abraham, and threw it away then so that it clattered on the stones, and ran off barefoot up the shore and on to the mountain.

A case of possession, or madness, whatever you want to call it. These things occur, among a crew of men alone in the North or on the deep ocean as they do here in our English towns and villages. What I mean to tell you is that it was Thomas Cave who brought him back. Cave did not let him go on alone but followed at a calm pace. There was visibility enough that day just to make out the two men on the mountainside, no more, no detail: two moving figures against the grey stillness of the rock, climbing, turning, tacking upwards, the Biscayan in a strange panicky rush that we could see even at that distance, Cave slow behind him, deliberate. Cave never once lost track of him though sometimes he took an entirely different path, switching back and working round where the madman scrabbled up too-sheer walls or unsafe shale in such a hectic way that to us observing below it seemed at times a wonder, or a symptom of the demonic nature of his possession, that he did not fall.

Cave caught up with him at last on a ledge overlooking the sea. We could not see what passed between them, only that they were still for a long time and that at last they turned and began a slow descent in single file. When the Biscayan got back to us he seemed to have forgotten all that occurred and followed Cave quiet as a lamb.

'What did you do?' we asked Cave.

'I read to him.'

He took out his Bible which he had carried inside his jacket.

'It is your Bible, not his. He is a Roman.'

'That need not matter.'

'What passage did you read him?'

'Whatever page I opened at.' He shrugged. 'A genealogy. It had no meaning for him, he does not understand the English. It would not matter if it were a Bible or a book of tides.'

Men spoke in whispers for fear the sound would carry in the sharpness of the clearing air.

'Before God, how can this be?'

'How is it that he has done such a thing, this man whom we all knew as no more than an ordinary man, like as not to any one of us? How was that that he alone of all of us could drive this devil out?'

'He came down from the mountain so calm and easy, as if he would have us think that nothing had occurred.'

'He has some power. He hides it from us.'

'Did you hear what he said? He said it would not matter if it were a book of tides from which he read. Did he dare to do this thing without the help of God?'

'No,' I said, 'it is not that. It is just that the man does not know English, that it matters not what words they were but what words he believed them to be.'

I thought it wrong that they talked so, that such suspicion might surround an act of goodness which we had each one of us observed. I did not like the direction in which their words tended. Questions passed from man to man, spun amongst us like the strands of the thinning mist.

'He knows something about this place that we do not know, something that allowed his survival.'

'No ordinary man could have lived that winter through. Didn't we all say that from the first?'

'Then how?'

'There is some power in this beyond nature.'

'And consider, the extraordinary stillness of the air these past days, is that also of nature?'

'It gives a man the need to pray.'

I heard it said that it was Cave who had held us there

beyond our time of departure, that it was in his power to call the winds to take us away. There was a whisper even, light as vapour and I could not say from whom it had come, that the lost boat was bewitched by him.

Even when we set sail these thoughts did not die but surrounded Cave and kept him apart.

England

20

A SLUGGISH SEA, a smear of green, a grey rivermouth that we rode up with the tide. It was many years since Cave had set foot in his native land but he did not say how many.

I had thought that England would make him glad. Yet I saw no sign of it, no expression on him but a kind of vague bewilderment. I saw him on the gangplank, he was so tall and spare that he made a distinct figure among those who surrounded him, and he stood and hesitated a moment as if he must build up nerve for what would follow. And then he gave a kind of shrug, and stretched that long body that had been cramped up so many days on the ship, and stepped down on to the crowded quay. For some way his head showed above the level of the crowd, and he broke a passage through it with determined strides so that the world seemed to ripple back and did not touch him.

So it was wherever he went in the months that followed. He held himself intact from men and none came close to him. I can say this because I spent more time with him than anyone. For some months I travelled and lived with him and yet even I could not have said truthfully that I knew him, that I knew what went on within him, though I observed him closely, with the kind of close and superficial attention a boy will give to a man who might be his model or his hero, though I could have enumerated so many of the little intimacies of his life, what were his tics of manner, how he chewed his meat and when his bowels moved, the way his fingers quivered as they reached for his fiddle or hovered about the narrow bowl of his pipe, how he slept with a thin snore and mutterings that sometimes seemed so coherent that I looked for meaning in them, only they were in no language that I have heard before or since.

It was because of the Captain that I went with him. But for Captain Marmaduke I think that Cave would have vanished then and there from my life, striding out of it with the barrel of heels to sell, and his chest and his violin and his wager. His story would have remained as a curious memory, no more, maturing into something distant and half-believed like a myth. I would not have come back to puzzle over him after twenty years, nor been driven as I was last summer to leave my home for a time and attempt to seek him out.

When the cargo was dispersed each man of the crew came to the *Heartsease* – an ill name it had become – to collect the share that was due to him and take his leave of the Captain, who had remained black with grief in his cabin all the time since we had come in and scarcely set foot ashore. For Thomas Cave there was the money from the wager, that we had signed for all of a long year before, in addition to his pay from this voyage and what I had held for him from the previous one: some considerable wealth this was, all in all, though you would not have thought it for the meagre look on him. The Captain in parting asked what he would do with it and Cave answered only that it would take him home, and spoke the word like it was a strange and surprising destination.

'In Heaven's Name, man, it will take you farther than that!' said the Captain, waking for a moment from his sad stupor, and Cave said only yes, that he trusted so.

There was a pause between them then, each man lost once more in some grim thought of his own, and then the Captain came back to himself and reached out his hand to Cave and said that he was a brave man and wished him luck.

Then his eye chanced on me and it seemed that he spoke on impulse: 'Take the boy with you, Thomas, as he's headed in the same direction.' I think that it was a kind of care for me because I made him think of Edward. And he pointed out a ship that was readying for Yarmouth and said that her master was a friend of his, and we were gone that same day.

We came to Yarmouth and then here to Swole, and for all that time there were others about us, sailors and a couple of others paying passage like ourselves, and Cave was shy amongst us. Once he heard me begin to tell the story of the wager, too loud I am sure, I was puffed up with the adventure though I had had in truth only the tiniest piece in it, and Cave interrupted me then and called me to him; and that was the only time that I can remember him taking an active part in our intercourse. I thought that he was to tell me off for giving away among strangers the knowledge of the money he carried, knowledge that might travel about him and bring the thieves on him when we touched land, but it was not that. No, he told me only but in hard terms that he would have me not speak any further word of what he had done, wager or no wager, nor even to suggest to any man that such a winter might be lived.

'Not a word, my boy, promise me that. Let no man conceive it possible, no man follow me there.'

'Why? Was it so terrible as that?'

'You misunderstand me,' he said, and there was a bitter note in his voice. 'It is not for the men I say this, but for the rest. Let the men look out for themselves.'

I confess that I was at first a little afraid of him. Not of any physical aspect of him, but of something else, what he was or what he knew. I was not altogether without superstition. Yet from Swole we went for two days on foot, the pair of us alone skirting the marsh and then cutting across the open heath going inland, and in that time we did not speak much, nor did he say anything particular to put my mind at rest, but only walked, and I learnt that there is no better companion-ship than to walk with a man, stride for stride. In the silence of walking I watched him, and as the hours and the miles passed my wariness faded, and I came to trust him, if for nothing more than the steadiness of his pace, which kept even throughout the day, and the wintry clarity of his eyes.

When we reached my home my family welcomed us with joy and tears, my little sister shot up like a woman and my mother crying at seeing another of her children being so grown and travelled. They took Cave in as my friend and he stayed with us till Christmas but soon as that day was passed he came to some silent decision, took up his few things and said that he would be gone.

My mother, who was a woman full of heart, took me aside.

'What great sorrow is it in your friend that he has no other person to hold to, that he broods so, all alone?'

I thought that good reason to break my promise, just this once, to my mother alone, and recounted to her the extraordinary tale of his hermitude.

'There's something more, something behind it all,' she went on, but I told her grandly that such was the life of the sea, that an adventurer such as Cave had seen more on this earth than a mere woman could possibly imagine, and she laughed and said what a man I had become, though she looked at me like I was still a child as she said it.

Later she came to me again, and she had packed some provisions, cheese and bacon, and told me that she could see what I wanted, that it would do no harm and might indeed be kindness to keep company with him a while more before I went back to sea.

'You do not have to go.' Cave hesitated as we walked away, looked at me and back at my family waving. 'Why not stay with them?'

'There are too many of us to make a living there.'

'There's other work besides the sea.'

'It's what I want.'

'What do you want?'

'To travel, see the world. You know how it is.'

'Do I?'

'Oh yes, sir. Think of all the places you and the others have told me of, the wonders in them. The Azores and the islands of the Indies, the forests of Virginia and the painted people there, the river big as a sea where Raleigh sailed in search of Eldorado. The beasts and creatures and coloured birds, the naked coal-skinned women whom they sell for slaves. I would not know about these things if you had not told me of them.'

'But those are only stories,' he said. 'You can hear them at home by the fire.'

I thought that odd in a man that had gone and seen so much as he.

Cave chose our way though I could not tell if there was sense in the road he took. In winter so much of the land looked alike, the stripped fields, the glassy river that spilled out across the meadows, the bent black arms of the trees, the holes and ruts that we must watch beneath our feet.

'Where do we go?' I asked.

He looked to the horizon. That's what Cave did, he looked to the horizon or he looked to the ground before him; his eyes rarely seemed to pause on the level between where they might meet another's.

'Will we go on now to the village that you come from?'

There was a hamlet that we passed through, early, so early that the day was only beginning in it. The steam of morning rose from the pig pens in the yards beside the road where we walked, rising into the cold air off the animals' backs as they came out to eat, and from the sheds behind came the lowing of cattle and the shuffle of milking.

Cave stood in the middle of the street and surveyed it, stood so still that the hens came and pecked about the mud where it was turned by his stick.

'Is this it? Are we there?'

He looked from one house to the next, at door and window and thatch and chimney, looked at the people who passed as if they also were made of wood and mud and straw. A cold drizzle had begun to fall and put their heads down so that they did not seem to see us. They were bleary anyway and blinkered before their work that time of day.

'Shall we stop?'

'No,' said Cave, 'it is too early to stop. We might do many miles today.' He wore no hat and already his hair and beard were dark with the rain and stuck about his face.

When I hesitated he said again, 'Let us go on. I have no business here.'

The rain fell harder as he spoke and the place seemed to contract before us. I was sure that this was it, this must have been his home, and I felt a terrible disappointment for him. It was so bleak and grey, and on this one morning most of all, full of blind bent people. I felt young as a child and helpless to speak, though all my nature wished to cheer him.

We had walked some way beyond the village when a cart

came up behind and because of the rain it picked us up. We sat in the back with a sack over our two heads and as long as the rain fell the carter barely spoke to us nor we to him. When the rain cleared he stopped for the horse to eat, and I remember that I thought to entertain the others by clowning on the grass. I used to do that in those days. I had quite a skill in tumbling, could have joined a fair, so people said. So I warmed myself and them by performing my repertory of tricks, and because the ground was wet I slipped and fell about this way and that, until they began to laugh.

When the cart went on, we talked. 'Where have you been?' the carter asked, and I thought that it was my chance now to impress him with stories of a frozen sea and mountains made of ice, great white bears and fish as big as houses.

But the man had travelled no further afield than Stowmarket and had never seen the sea. 'There are some big fish about, that's true. They do say you know there's a pike in the river here long as a horse. A great old beast with teeth like a saw. It'll swallow a duck whole, snatch it down in the water and swallow it, just like that.'

Then it rained again and we were back with the sack above our heads.

'I'm sorry, lad, I could not stop there this morning,' Cave said at last. 'Too much time had passed. The place was full of strangers. There was no purpose in my being there.'

I was so young then, bold, certain. 'But you cannot say that. You were hardly there a moment. And the people we saw, they'll be no other than the people that you knew grown older, or at least the children of the people that you knew. If you'd said who you were, someone would have known you for sure.'

Cave looked out along the road. His face bore a sheen of moisture from the rain.

Was it true, the reason he gave? I have thought many times about it in the years since then, what precisely it was drove Thomas Cave away: whether it was as he said, the strangeness of the place, or whether it was its very familiarity, that threatened somehow to close in on him.

I parted from him soon after, to make my way back to Swole. We had come to a place where the river became tidal and we could begin to smell the sea.

'Will you not come on a little further?' I asked, and Cave said no, that he had come far enough, and looked down to his feet on the fresh grass. He would keep to the land now. He was done with the sea. There was a church in that village with a roof like a barn and he laid his things down and his big cloak like a blanket and said that he would sleep in its porch.

At the last moment, in an entirely unexpected gesture, he spread his arms and hugged me, and in that touch I knew all of a sudden how great my affection for this man had grown. And then I turned as I must and left him in the porch, and walked out beneath the gulls and the wide sky.

'Lad,' he called, as I reached the gate. 'Take this. I have no need of so much.' He pulled out his purse from inside his shirt and gave me some coins from it, pressed them into my outstretched flushed hand with his own cold fumbling one. 'I insist.' Again but tremblingly we embraced, and I walked on two miles before the sun set behind me.

I knew nothing more of him for well on twenty years.

21

I T WAS ON a summer evening like this one that I first heard of Cave again. I had been here at Swole some years, living here. I must have been about the age that he was that long winter. It is a time when a man – a man like myself at any rate for I cannot begin to speak for him – knows the urge to settle and be with his family and feel the land beneath his feet.

I had found myself a wife and gone into business in association with my cousin who was at Aldborow, trading along the coast. Though it was hard – business has been hard these past years, the state of the country poor and nothing easy – it had gone well enough. The summer was fair, the evenings long and calm, and I had taken to spending them as I do this one, here before the shore. A finer time of day I cannot imagine, when the air is still and warm, and the light long, and the fishermen spread and stitch their nets, and the sun sets behind our backs while the sea slowly dulls before us. I was sitting pretty much as now, with my back to a flint wall, listening with only half an ear, watching the sea before me, watching the ships. Strange how you look out every now and then to see the passing ships, and it's so still on the shore that you think they must be fixed there, and yet you fill your pipe and look out again, and their positions have been rearranged though they have not appeared to move.

The talk was of a man who had knowledge of the North.

'Did you know him, Mister Goodlard? He must have been a whaler like yourself.'

I think that it was a moment before I took in the woman's question. I was watching the children run and play at the sea's edge. My own two were among them. They all ran into the waves and did not mind that they got wet because the water and the evening were warm.

'Could be this man was someone you had known?'

'Who's that?'

'The fishermen met a man down the coast, they said he had been a whaler.'

'What was his name?' I asked, and she said that she did not know his name.

I told her that the northern seas were huge and that there were on them a hundred whaleships from England alone. I could hardly be expected to know every man or every crew.

The woman talked on.

This man had ice in him, she said, a tall, thin, bent man with the cold sea in his eyes. He came to their villages alone and sudden like a late spring frost, and brought with him a chilly touch that stilled madmen, cooled women in the pangs of labour and dispelled pain in the dying. It was said that he had the power to drive out devils.

At first I thought nothing of it. There were so many stories. There were so many who wandered the country, and in these eastern counties they said more than anywhere, not only merchants and pedlars and vagabonds but men with ideas in their heads, all kind of preachers and healers and prophesiers, and every one of them with some story to tell of the strange and the magical and the unexplained. I had been out of England long. I cannot tell you how disconcerting it had been at first, how it had made me feel alone and a foreigner, coming home to my own land from years at sea to walk in the crowded street or sit here on the shore before the boats and hear such a bemusing mass of talk. But I had learnt to let it by, to smoke and look and nod and appear to listen, and not to give offence. So many speakers there were, so many extraordinary tales: how should I distinguish amongst them? How, in all of that garrulous discourse, should I pay attention to talk of one lone man?

My little girl fell on the beach but picked herself up laughing, such a sturdy rounded shape she was, and ran on up to me to brush the sand off her.

'I saw a fellow could be he,' said a fisherman. 'At Blythburgh, I think it were, not far off from here. Old, he was old as Moses, carried a stick and had few words about him as I could tell.'

There was an uncle of my wife's who lived in a village close to the marsh. He came by and stopped with us a night, and spoke of an exorcism that had taken place in that village the year before, a stranger who had appeared from the mist and saved a child and cast out a devil from a man possessed, and done it by some special magic and without recourse to the Name of God.

'What was he like, this man?'

'Old. A tall man grey and stiff like a piece of weathered oak. He made me afraid just to see him.'

'Did you learn his name?'

'If anyone learnt his name they did not say it. Seems he goes without names and pleasantries. No words to him that I heard.'

'And where does he live?'

It appeared that the man had vanished as mysteriously and suddenly as he had come, and because of this people were afraid and said when they saw lights that he was still out there with the spirits on the marsh. Our visitor did not give much credence to their talk. There were some who said the man had turned himself to vapour and blown back north from whence he came. 'No such magic to him, I'll reckon. There's many like him, has the knack of turning a spirit, but he'll have a trade too, no doubt, he'll just have wandered on, and because the mist was in none noted where he went.'

'No, indeed,' said I, but as he spoke the memory had come back to me of Cave and the Biscayan's fit of madness.

For the first time I asked myself if it were possible that Cave were still alive. It could be so, I thought. A man who had honed his endurance to such a degree might well live long.

★   ★   ★

For some days after he had left I thought on this and my preoccupation must have showed.

'What is it troubles you?' my wife asked me.

'It sounds as if this was a good man, this man you knew,' she said, when I had told her everything. 'How foolish men are to be afraid of someone like that, just because he does what they cannot do or explain. There is so much that we must accept and that cannot be explained, we cannot be always making conspiracy or judgement over it. For sure you must go, if you once cared about him, find this man my uncle spoke of and see if he is the same. I see that you will have no rest until you do find out and it is settled.'

There are not many women would be so understanding.

The children climbed on me as I took my leave. My daughter cried that she did not want her father gone off again to sea. 'But I shan't be at sea, my sweet,' I said. 'This time all my journey will be on land, and I shall be back before you know it.'

The village was a small place at the edge of the estuary where the marsh gives way to the farmland, where you can stand beneath the height of the church and turn one way to see tilled fields and the other to see a salty wilderness. I went there and asked about the story he had told us.

There was an old man who had a bench before his house on which he sat all through the day. His eyes were beginning to cloud and grow milky but he could still observe well enough.

It was a sailor, this man said, who had come back from distant parts; he could not say where, only that he had been in some piracy or battle there and become horribly disfigured, with an arm cut off at the elbow and a sword slash across his face, so that the sight of him brought fear to the minds of his children who did not know him and ran away. His wife recognised him despite his awful wounds, and took him in and called the children back, and cooked his meals and made his home about him. But the sailor could not settle, and whatever horrors he had seen came back and raged before his eyes, until one day he fell into a fever and began to scream and rave with such violence that his wife became frightened of him and ran off to ask others for help. And almost all of the village came by, those who wished to help and those who were just curious, and when he saw at his door the crowd come to stare at him as if he were not himself, not a man of the village but some exotic alien creature, the poor sailor went quite mad. There was a baby in the house, a youngest child born to them even while he was away at sea, and the moment he opened his door and met the crowd of villagers, the baby began to cry. A great, ear-splitting squawl it was, that rang out through the village, as if the baby understood all the danger of the moment, and the sailor went quite mad and snatched it up.

The old man said this, and more, but I had better details later from the woman herself when I went to seek her out. The sailor now that I met him seemed a silent, sulky fellow who could remember nothing, but the woman could tell it all like it was happening again immediately before her eyes: her husband's wild look, the stupidity of the villagers like a herd of staring, snuffling heifers, the sudden rending sound of the baby's cry.

'Oh, sir, you would remember that cry if you had heard it. Even if you had been a mile away.'

She was standing at the side of the door, suddenly alarmed at the attention she had brought to the house but unable now that she had called the others to fend them off. She saw the look of rage come into her husband's face, saw him grab up in his one hand the bundle of the squawling baby, stood by powerless as he shouldered through the passive crowd, like a battering ram pushing them aside, and ran out into the village street and to the church at the edge of the marsh.

They saw him next on top of the tower. The baby was still screaming and its noise carried down to them from the height and spread like the sound of bells. It was a great high tower with a parapet cut like a castle wall. He stood close against this and yelled down at the crowd, holding the writhing baby beneath his arm and leaning over so that at any instant they feared that it might struggle from his grip and drop down into the churchyard beneath. And then he swung one leg over the flint parapet where it faced the marsh, and in the awful hush of a moment they thought that he would jump.

'It was the Devil in him,' the woman said.

She looked up to where her baby cried, up the tower with the sky bright and white above it.

'It was not him my husband there, I swear, but the black figure of Beelzebub. Thin, horrid, weirdly hunched, a black shape that it did hurt the eyes to see. It was the Devil and not any form of man.' The poor woman paused and clenched herself, and looked to me for reassurance before she could continue. 'And this creature did put his leg over the parapet and sit astride it, as a man does on a horse, and set to rocking back and forth as if the horse were galloping, back and forth, the Devil galloping away up there with my baby under his arm. The Lord is my witness, that is how I saw it. Ask others here if they did not see the same.'

And I did ask others, and all whom I met in the village concurred that this was how it seemed.

All of that day and through the night the madman rode the parapet. The stars came out, and a moon just full enough to make out the shape like an excrescence on the tower. The baby was silent a long time and then set to whimpering, long slow waves of whimpering that ran on like the gusts of wind through the reeds. The woman stood below, and others with her, only the ones who cared now for the mere spectators had grown bored and gone home asking to be called again if any change occurred. What change could there have been, she asked, but the final drop, the image of which ran and reran vividly before her watching eyes, so fast it would occur that she knew there would be nothing for them to see, no action, no occurrence but only its consequence: a flicker before the eye and then on the ground a misshapen tiny bundle of blood-spattered cloth. So fast it could occur and at any instant that she could not bear for any amount of time to look away. All through the night she kept vigil, and the parson and the others kept up beside her, praying. For so long she stood looking up that her neck and back and the calves of her legs shot through with pain.

In the morning the sun rose on the silver estuary and he

had not moved. There was no whimpering, no wind, no sound that reassured of the continuance of life. All that day he held there, and another night.

The second dawn a tall man came into the village. Streaks of pink sky behind him, a soft threat of rain. The man walked with a stick as he had a slight limp. He made his way to the churchyard and announced to those who waited there that he had been told to come. His pale eyes glanced up to the parapet where the sailor still sat with his one hand clasping the bundle to his chest, his body swaying gently now as if with a breeze, his face raised to the fine drizzle that had begun to fall.

'How long's he been there?'

'Two nights,' the woman said. Her voice was stiff from the silence.

'May I see if I may help?'

'If you can deal with devils. It is the Devil in him, for sure. The man he is would never, could never, do such a thing.'

The stranger's look was quite without alarm. 'Mistress, you would be surprised what a simple man can do.'

And the parson held open the heavy wooden door of the church but none of the others would enter with him.

They moved away then, stood down by the churchyard gate with the road and the village like safety at their backs. They saw the head of the stranger emerge on the far side of the tower and hold still for a long while. The rain intensified and the scene on the tower became no more than a blur, the man on the parapet a vague solid against the mist. The rain poured into their upturned eyes. 'My baby,' the woman cried all of a sudden, a piercing scream that must have risen shrill to the tower, 'Save my baby!' and threw herself down thrashing on the muddied ground. Just at that moment those who still looked up saw a puff of smoke as from an explosion and a strange black bird, long and ungainly in the start of its flight as a heron, take off from the tower into the raincloud. Or so they said later. They said it was the Devil.

And the stranger came down from the tower and with him the sailor whose body trembled all over and whose face was white like lard. The woman grabbed the baby from his arms, and its cheeks were cold in the rain but it reached out feeble hands to her and she gave it her breast to suck and she was bursting with milk. The stranger stood apart and none approached him. The people were more afraid of him than of the other man who seemed now so pale and broken and without power.

'What can I give you?' the woman asked, but her eyes were all for the child, the mouth latched on to her, the eager eyes and outstretched tiny fists as it revived.

'Nothing,' he said. 'You can give me nothing.'

And as he went to the churchyard gate the cluster of people parted wide to let him through, and the villagers who had come out of their houses stood back as he limped away and out of sight.

22

I TOLD MY WIFE.
'I feel sure that it was he.'

My little girl was too lively on my knee, wriggling, pulling at my beard, turning until her thicket of hair was before my eyes. Her mother sat solemn, waiting for what I had to say, but my talk was all disjointed.

'It would be too great a coincidence that it could be any other. No, I believe that it is him and that he is alive to this day.'

'Did no one give you hint of where to find him?'

'No one seemed to know. In your uncle's village they said only that he went into the marsh. In other places where I think he might have been men said he left to go inland, or to the coast, that he had come from Bury or they had heard of him at Lowestoft, that he was gone into Norfolk or south to Ipswich or to quite other parts. Then a man would mention a little event that happened somewhere or other, that might have been him, somewhere quite close, and I would follow this up and it would yield nothing and I would find only another story to take its place. It became hopeless. For many days I heard only gossip and rumour. Every fact that might be in it seemed embroidered, there was so little that I could recognise as truth.'

'Poor Tom, so you have been gone for nothing then? But it was important to you.'

'Sometimes it has come so that I have wished I had never begun it. You do not know, living here with the family about you in this one place where you belong, you do not know how it is out there. There is unreason, anger and madness in the world that I do not understand.'

When we were alone and the children gone to bed, I told her how on my way back I had stopped at a ramshackle village inn and found people talking in a fever about some witchcraft that had been done there and how a woman and a man were to be put to the test that next day and swum in the pond before the green.

'It was the kind of story, Mary, that one has heard too many times: a woman who lived alone and was wanton and had a dispute with her neighbour. She had taken in a man and it was said that these two together had persecuted the neighbour and sent an imp to stampede his cattle, and bewitched his cart so that four horses could not move it, even making one of the horses to kick his pregnant wife in the stomach – all such circumstantial nonsense as common-sense would see through in a minute, and yet I was interested, because the man that was with her, that they blamed for at least the half of this, they described as an itinerant shoemaker but eerie, and old enough to be her father. So I stayed the night in the village, with just the possibility in my mind that this could be Cave, and the village was a dismal place, even in summer, set up alone and exposed, and nowhere better for me to sleep but this same flea-ridden inn.'

'And was it him?'

Excitement in her question, yet it was a time before I could bring myself to tell it all. So soft it was there, sitting in the house with the light failing outside, with Mary's face half shadowed across the table and the children sleeping silent on their beds in the other room through the open door. There was such peace and innocence in the moment that I was reluctant to bring into it the ugly scene.

One of the children stirred and a blanket fell to the floor. Mary went and settled them and sat there a few minutes, and I recall that I got up and paced about, and came back and sat again as I had all the evening. I did not speak until she was back beside me. I knew that her eyes were on me though it had become dark.

'I will tell you what I witnessed, as it did meet my eyes. I cannot say how it might have seemed to me if I had only come by idly and happened upon it. If I had but chanced by, then I might perhaps have thought it, as others did, a diversion and a spectacle. But you know what thoughts were in my mind, and because of these what I saw seemed only cruel and evil.

'It was a pretty day, even in that dreary place, and the whole village came out to watch, and maybe people from other villages roundabouts, because I would not have thought those few hovels could have produced such a crowd: men, women, children, all out on the green as if it there was a fair coming, seated on the grass and plucking daisies between their fingers. And then this wagon came through and they stood and jeered, and as I was away at the back I could not see well, and there was a tall man in black like a preacher or a justice, and two dishevelled figures were unloaded from the wagon, a plump woman and a thin and white-haired man, conspicuously tall though he was bent with age – and at that distance, Mary, and with so many standing between us, I could not have said if he was or was not Cave or any man that I might or might not once have known.

'I pushed through the crowd and made my way down to the edge of the pond, and by that time they had stripped the pair of their outer clothing and tied their thumbs and toes together and were throwing them into the water. Just bundles they seemed, but the woman screamed plenty, and the crowd yelled behind me. A horrid bullying, it was. Devil's whore, they called her, and other such things. See, they shouted out, there's proof. She floats like a plank. I could not have said if she floated or no, for she was fat and the water was shallow, and they pulled her out so muddy that you might have thought her behind had rested on the bottom. And the man had scarcely been in time enough to sink, and yet they pulled him out also.

'I saw his face then, and he was not my Thomas Cave. Just some piteous old man, all wet, and staring and shivering like a trapped hare. And I left then and came directly home. I did not have the heart to see more.'

★   ★   ★

That night I had a troubling dream.

I dreamt that I was back there in the North. It was late in the season. I knew that because ice already closed the bay. I knew that I was stranded, a prisoner for the winter though there were no walls or bars to my prison but only an endless space cut about by wind. I stood with my back to the mountains and with the sea of ice ahead, and the wind came down between the peaks and whipped hard-formed grains of snow in waves along the ground and past my feet. In the distance this driven snow seemed like a knee-high flood swirling above the surface of the beach and the frozen sea.

And then I saw men coming towards me as if they were floating, though I understood that they were walking with their boots obscured in the snow. Three men in tall black hats, taking form out of the distance, strangely tall because of their hats and because their feet did not appear to touch the ground. They passed so close that I saw the knuckles of their hands and the lines of their faces, but they did not seem to see me and went directly to the tent where Thomas Cave lived, which was close by though I had not noted it before.

When they came out two of the men dragged Cave between them. They had tied him about the arms and the ankles with rope so that he could not walk but barely hobble. They took him to a point out on the ice and their leader made a hole in it with the staff he carried, working it around like an auger until the hole was large enough to take a man. And they threw Cave in head first and then turned their backs and walked away.

By the time I got to him the ice was frozen over again like glass, and its transparency was such that I could see him in the clear blue water beneath. He held his hands to his sides and swam with all his body like a seal, his uncut hair flowing out and his beard dividing like a fork beneath his chin, his tied legs making his feet into a seal's tail. He dived down deep, and seals came up from below to play with him. I cried out but he could not hear me under water, and I hammered with my boot on the ice to break it but it only became the thicker and more opaque.

When I knew I was awake, I was shivering. My wife wrapped the blankets about us and held me tightly to give me warmth. She said that she had never felt a man so cold.

She put her hand warm to my lips and quieted my cry. 'Shhh,' she said. 'Do not let the children wake. Breathe slow and let the warmth spread through you, and then tell me what you have seen.'

It seemed a long time before I could find words. I heard the rustle of the bedding heavy as if it were canvas, heard the children's sleeping breaths loud and insistent, heard the bark of a dog outside and its cry carried by other dogs about the town, every sensation heightened and only slowly fading into ordinariness.

At last I told her that it was my horror in my dream that I could not break through and save him.

Again she put a finger to my panicked lips.

'Coming back to us does not mean that you have abandoned your search, only that you do not know where else to look. So go no further. Continue your search instead from here if you must. See who comes by and talk to them, and when you travel somewhere, then speak to men there also. Open the subject and tell the story of his winter in the North. Say that he came back here, and see then what others have to offer. If he is alive and in the district, sooner or later you will find him out.'

23

A FULL YEAR it took. And then this summer when I
was down the coast I met a reed cutter who had news
that I believed. He said that he knew the man of whom I
spoke, and had seen where he lived on the edge of the marsh
where a village had once been lost to the sea. There were just
a couple of huts left of the village and this old man was the
only resident, living alone with the marsh behind and the sea
before him and no other habitation for miles.

I asked where, and how far, and he gave me good
directions. I never saw a plainer, more practical-looking
fellow than this reed cutter, blue-eyed, ruddy-faced, all the
redder because the day was hot and he was sweating,
standing steady on his boat that was piled so thick across
with reeds that it seemed solid as an island. I untied the rope
that moored him and helped him push away.

'You'll be going down to see him?'

'Why, yes,' I said, 'I will.'

'They do say things about him, you know. You can't put

too much store on it, the world's full of nervous, chattering folk saying this and that and all kind of nonsense, but then you can't be sure either. A man who can do what he does, his cures and such, you never know where it ends, do you?'

He said one other thing that made me shiver.

He told me he had heard it said that the old man had two creatures he kept by him, that some folk said were his familiars – one of them a fox with fur as white as snow and the other an immaculate white bird that had a cry like a shriek of anger – and these were seen about him in the winter and when the sea mists spread inland.

'How can this be?' I asked. 'I know these beasts by your description but they are none that belong here.'

He said that he could only repeat what he had heard, and I wondered at it. For it seemed to me that these were beasts from the whale stations: the beautiful but raucous snowbird, and the northern fox whose fur turns white to blend with the snow. Was it possible that some other whaler had come by and spoken of them, and the ideas had somehow linked in people's minds? If not, then I could not think by what coincidence or suggestion these Suffolk villagers might have dreamt such creatures up.

I went to find him that last week of July. It was the hottest week of all this year. A day of high summer, the tidal mud shimmering in the sunlight and a flutter of birds in the reeds and along the creeks. I walked from inland where the reed cutter had said there was a path. He said that if I were to have gone by boat then sure the old man would see me approaching and vanish before I landed.

An unmarked sky wide as over sea. The marsh wide also, and flat. I had thought that the land I came off was flat but looking back from the edge of the marsh I saw how it rose behind me, how the horizon rose and bore the softness of trees in all directions save that of the sea. It was a place in which a man might well disappear, his tracks fine as those of an animal weaving along the edge of the reeds. All about me the stifling rustle of reeds, the whistle and piping of hidden birds. The path was not clear, it was so rarely used, though once or twice I found a few blackened boards set above the mud. On these boards my steps made reassuring hollow thuds. Twice I strayed and found myself stopped before an impassable channel: path gone, a creek before me, coppery water and polished mud. I must track back and find the way again and hope that I held my bearings.

At last I saw the hut, on a raised slip of land just visible above the reeds. A low hut of daub, a new reed thatch gleaming in the sunshine.

And there he was, sitting on a stool with his back to the wall and his eyes closed to the sun. It was him. I knew him at once. It was as if he had only greyed and dried in all the time since we last met, his hair and beard become thin grey strands, the skin of his face and hands like parchment and deeply drawn with lines. His eyes when he opened them were still strikingly pale and clear, but so transparent and without recognition that for a moment I wondered if they saw me.

'Thomas Cave.'

His long fingers groped as if for a thought and his brow narrowed in concentration.

'It's Tom Goodlard. It's me. Don't you know me? I see that I am much changed. I think I did not even have a beard when you saw me last.'

The hut seemed no more than a temporary shelter, its fresh thatch and the patches of new daub rough attempts to hold back the ruin that had come to the others that had stood beside it, wrecks with walls like broken hulls and rafters spillikined about them. No intention to permanence in it, as if it would take only a great wind and a rainstorm to tear and melt it down, or a wave to bite at the sandy cliff so close in front and give it to the sea like the rest of the village that was once there; as if it might be gone with the first storm of autumn, or the work of a winter at most. And yet the reed cutter had said that he had been here years; and there was wood cut and stacked, and lobster-pots beside the door, and in a hollow a heap of discarded crab and cockle shells.

Inside was a single stark room: a table with two loose-paged and broken books upon it; a cot with a once-coloured embroidered cloth swagged above its head, quite dirtied and faded with the years; the smell of old man and of fish.

I saw that his violin stood propped in a corner and was glad at that.

'You know that your cabin is still there?'

'Is that so?' Cave's words were flat and slow and I could not hear the thinking in them.

'Or it was, six or seven years ago when I went there last, and I cannot imagine things have changed since then.'

'You are still at the whaling then?'

'Not now, not for these past three years. I did well enough out of it in the end, put money by, came back here to live at Swole.'

'Not far from here.'

'No, not far.'

Cave pointed to the stool before the table, brought in from outside the only other one he had so that we might both be seated. He did not speak but placed gnarled hands between his knees and looked ahead as if he were still an old man alone.

'There's not so many goes to Duke's Cove any more, not that I know of anyhow. Not to the island, which they now call Edge Island, to any of those eastern islands and inlets. They say it's too risky, too much chance of getting beset with ice, if the season runs late and the winds turn; they say there's whales enough and safer hunting along the inlets of the western coast and have built there great cookeries for the oil. It's different now, it seems to me, they're different men.' I ran on and saw that he watched my lips as if he were reading them and still he did not speak. I thought that he took in what I said but I could not tell whether it interested him or not. 'It's changed from those first days of the *Heart-sease*. You'd be amazed to see it. The place hasn't changed of course, men can't touch that, but the business has, it's all very organised nowadays, big fleets from the big chartered Companies, a big trade.'

The window in the far wall had a view down on the

beach where the tide was almost at its last ebb, thin waves pulling away from stones on the wet sand. I could see among these stones recognisable pieces of houses: lintels, hearths, clusters of flints and of thin red bricks; pieces of the village that was lost. Still I was compelled to speak, rattling on to fill his silence. 'The Dutchmen,' I said, 'have built themselves a great town on the shore of the main island, before the largest of the bays, a town that has a population of many thousands in the season, a makeshift smoking factory town that has the name of Smeerenberg. It is such a big town now that it has its own cemetery, as any town must, an island they call Deadman Island, where bodies are carried by boat and, because the ground is too frozen beneath for digging, left in coffins heaped with piles of stones or wedged in between in the rocks, and even so the bears get to them. The bodies in that place do not rot from one season to the next, but dry and thin and whiten like beachcombings.'

'We should not have gone there.'

'What?' The interruption came soft as a breath. I could scarcely be sure that it was meant for me.

'We men. Any men. We should not have gone there. We should have left it be.'

The words came out in little runs, strange and hoarse but gathering power as if he had lost the habit of speech and just found it again, and now that they came he remembered hospitality and took up a flagon from the floor, and mugs, and laid them on the table.

'It was not right. I am sure of that now. We went where God did not mean us to go. We went beyond Him.'

'But we won't be there for ever. They say that those seas will be fished out, sometime soon, in a decade or half a century. You can see that, every year that passes, the whales are fewer, no longer those great heaving herds that filled the bays; some, but fewer, trailing in, and we must sail further for them, chase them out to the open sea. Sooner or later it'll end and we'll be gone, and the place will be lonely as it ever was.'

'But not the same.'

'What do you mean?'

'It will be changed, won't it? Just because we were there. Never the same.'

Cave slammed his mug down on the table so that the ale spilt out of it and wet his fingers.

'It was free of us, before. Now, because of us, things have been seen, heard there, that should never have been.'

We went out after that. It was too uneasy, sitting stiff at the table with that odd, hoarse speech echoing into the room. He stood slowly, unfolding himself as if he were brittle, and took up his stick and led me to where he had built a ladder against the precarious sand of the cliff and we went down and walked the beach. The sun was hot, the waves soothed as they pulled back against the shore. Thomas Cave lifted his head and sighed. I gave him my arm, for I could see that the stick was little support in the sand. His touch was dry and tentative like that of a moth. And after a moment he began to talk again, and this time his voice was quite different, thin but liquid and fluent.

Now I had the story off him, not of his winter on the

island, I think he will never tell that, but of the time since his return.

'Remember where you left me, in that river valley in the spring? I watched you go, watched a long way for I was tempted to follow. It seemed a long time until the sun set that evening, and not a soul came by after you had left me and I slept in the porch of the church and did not see nor spoke to anyone, and left in the morning early going back inland in the opposite direction to that by which you had gone, a bright morning it was and I had the sun behind me. So many mornings in those years I spent in that way, on the road with the sun low in a coloured sky, already walking out as some village wakes, walking through that bustling early time when the animals are brought out and the carts begin to pass and men set out for the fields. I stopped in a place, a town, a city, some lodging, and set up my craft with the tools I carried and worked for a time, for there was always work for me, leather to be found and feet to be shod, and people came to know me and I them, and soon as things became close I found that I must move on. Perhaps I had spent too many years already on the move. Or perhaps . . .'

He paused. His mouth was dry. He slapped his lips together and swallowed, closing his eyes a moment to the bright noon light.

'Or perhaps it was that I had set so still all of that year beforehand, that I had spent the winter as if in a prison.' When he opened his eyes they seemed somehow naked, the

228

pupils down to points and the colour drained out of them. 'Whatever the cause, the fact was so: I found that I could not settle in any one place on the land but was always restless. To stay somewhere had me frustrated as if becalmed, the place becoming oppressive to me, my thoughts becoming caged and pacing in my head and at last driving me on. I was in Halesworth, Bury, Cambridge, lost myself a long time in the wilderness of the fens, saw the great cathedrals of Ely and Lincoln and Norwich. I must have seen all the towns of eastern England, excepting the ports. I did not go to the ports. For many years I did not even go to the sea. For many years it went on like this, so long that I found that I had walked in circles and come back to places where I had been before, and people recognised me and asked me again to make for them, or do repairs, or help them with some other matter. I knew some cures, you see, and had learnt others from those that I met. I had herbs that I gathered as I travelled and I knew how to use them. In time my reputation as a healer became such that people would send to find me for this and not only for my trade, even at times pursuing me from far afield. As you have.'

And he lifted his hand from my arm and stared at me then. 'Why? What do you want of me?'

'I wanted nothing of you Thomas but to see you again.' I feared that I had lost his trust.

He is old, I thought. This heat will be too much for him and there is no shade. The beach ran featurelessly ahead, featurelessly behind, the low unstable cliff of shingle and sand, the shingle and the sand beneath it, the white fringe of waves, the shining sea. Perhaps it was time we turned back; I thought that he would want then to turn back but he did not. He put his hand back to my arm and took up his pace again and his story.

'These are disturbing times we live in now. I sometimes think that we are on the edge of tumultuous times. Have you noted how many strange events occur, the storms we've had, the floods, the strange kinds of hail and rain, the thunder unseasonal in midwinter, the snow in spring? And other things beyond the weather: was it last year or the year before, one year not long past, a crash in the heavens and a raining of stones from the sky, not hailstones these but rock, some hard rock of a colour like metal that none had ever seen before, and then one single stone the size of a loaf and hot to the touch, falling on to the heath before the town of Woodbridge? Myself I cannot suggest any cause for this, save only the idea of some physical change or realignment in the heavens, but there are many who see other meanings in it all, omens and judgements and warnings, and are made fearful and thrown into ferment.

'I cannot say when it began precisely, or how, only that the people who came to me began to ask for other things. They saw something in me besides the cures that I had done, saw what perhaps they sought to see, what I can only explain as a reflection of their fear and their incomprehension. They began to say that I had powers.' He spoke the last word with a strange emphasis, his eyes wide like innocence in the old parchment of his face.

'I do not have powers, Tom Goodlard, believe me.

'I do what I do, that is all. I have experience and I use a few herbs such as could be found by any man or woman who has the sense to look. I speak to men and I appeal to them with reason. And that is all there is to it. Anything else is lies and fancy. What did they tell you of me, those who told you where to find me? What did they say?'

'That you had been North and that you travelled about. I guessed that it was you from the description. There are not so many of us whalemen hereabouts.'

'And what else? What was it made them speak of me to you?'

'That, and also that you saved a man, and I remembered how something like it occurred with one of the men from the *Heartsease* there on the island shortly before we left.'

I saw at once that I should not have said that. What better thing I could have said though I do not know. Now again he doubted me. His face clammed tight although his touch remained on mine. I left the words time to fade. We walked on until we reached a wide creek where we had no choice but to turn. For the first time we could see the world of men beyond the marsh: the roofs of a village and a church tower in the distance. We walked back the way we had come, only the sea was on our left now and the sun was in our faces and dazzling.

'They say I cast out devils, don't they? And perhaps you have said it also. No, do not deny it.'

The sun was too bright for him and he looked at the ground as he walked, down at the broken shells and the high-tide debris at his feet. He seemed so old in that bright light that I felt tender to him.

'Do you know what else they say?' he went on. 'You must have heard what else they say. They say that because I seem to have the power to drive out devils I myself am some kind of witch. What fools we have in the world.'

A large bird wheeled over the sea, over our heads. Snow-white feathers, and a shadow passed over me. But when it turned I saw that its back was grey: it was only a common gull, of which there must be a million down this coast.

'You have found a good place here, Thomas Cave. You will be safe here.'

'Safe? From what must I be safe?'

'From devils. From harm. From those fools you speak of.'

We parted beneath the cliff. No white birds here but swallows, a flock of them darting in and out of the nests they had in its pitted side. Thomas Cave offered me one last piece of himself.

'If there was one thing I learnt in the North, Tom Goodlard, it was this: that there are no devils out there. No devils in the ice or the snow or the rocks, none but those inside us, those we bring. That is why they can be dispelled, because they are all in our imaginations; how could it happen otherwise? They can be dispelled because they are not there, because they are no more than words, dreams, pictures in the mind.'

I think that was his drift, so far as I could follow it. I am a simple man. I know nothing of imagination. I know no more than what I can see and hear, and what is in the Testaments. Cave spoke of things that went beyond me.

'Think of that place before we got there, lad.' He called

me that as if he had forgotten that I was grown, had me there again a boy at his side. 'Think of it before Barents, before Marmaduke, before any man stepped upon it. Only the place and the surprising abundance of Nature in it. So cold, so inhospitable it looked to us, but in the season so much lived there. The whales, the seals, the birds, so many birds, like these swallows here. In its cold way it was a paradise. No man there, no devils, nor even, I came to think, a God, or not any God that we know. Only itself. And then we came. We came with our killing and our fear and saw devils there. Did you never think that? Did you never look at it? Never once stand back, when it was so bright about us, and see it, the horror of it, the blood that stained the sea, the grease and smoke, the violation? Did you never have the urge to run off into the whiteness, into the ice, dissolve into it, wipe yourself clean? Now that I am old I have that feeling again and again. I have it when I look at the sea. I stand here with my back to the cliff and the works of men behind me, and I look at the sea and at the waves coming in, and hope that my soul will merge with it and be washed away.'

What could I say to that? Such fluent intensity in his voice, and his meaning flying out somewhere just beyond my comprehension.

I spoke my farewell in common and mundane terms, the only words that were available to me, and found my path home.

24

THEY STILL SPEAK of him in the Greenland seas. Of Cave, or I think it is Cave, and his endurance. It is as if the memory of him were frozen, preserved like everything else, only thinned and refined over time, worn down by the wind and ice, so that he becomes less and less a real man that others once sailed with, and more a figment of their minds.

Sometimes his name is changed or lost, and he becomes a Dane or a Dutchman and no longer an Englishman, and yet it is surely his lone ordeal that is remembered and embroidered and retold. I have heard it in many places from men of different ships and different nations: that years back, at the beginning of the trade, a man had wintered on the shore alone, and the reasons they give for this are various. Some have said that he acted out of his own inexplicable will, others that it was fate alone and that he was cast away by chance, yet others that he had an evil spirit in him and was left a Jonah by his shipmates who were fearful of his presence on the voyage home. Many things are said, some approaching the truth and some far from it and laughable. I heard one story that when his ship returned he had written a fine poem of a hundred stanzas and set it to music, another that out there on the snow he had fought a great white bear with his own hands, and though he bore for the rest of his life the stripes of its claws across his face, he had at last tamed it so that it followed him like a dog and came to its name, and he fed it fish and tidbits of seal.

There are other men who have attempted to repeat his action, not lone men so far as I know but whalecrews who by mischance or to stake their company's claim have stayed back to pass the winter on the ice. And though one year or two they have succeeded, the half of them have perished, and these dead men have left the log of their dying beside their scurvied and frozen bodies. I have heard sailors say that it is a horror to come upon them, to see their hollow staring eyes.

Once, in the early days, when all the different nations were first competing for the whaling grounds and stations, the Muscovy Company of London obtained a band of condemned criminals and brought them north, and offered them their reprieve if they would overwinter and hold the ground for the next season. The men worked the summer alongside the regular sailors, and at the end of it when the ship was readied to leave they were supplied with all the necessary provisions and the promise of generous pay to follow, besides their pardon. And as the last boat pushed out they looked about them and felt the breath freeze in their nostrils. They cried out and called the boat back. They begged the captain to put them again into their chains and take them home. They would not stay. No, for fear. Rather the company of men and the sentence that awaited them, even if this were hanging.

There was something there that they dreaded more than death. What was it? I ask you. Was it the ice or the unknown, the sheer unnamedness of the place? Or was it the solitude?

Even now after so many years, I can close my eyes and bring looming from the darkness the image of Thomas Cave as we left him, as the *Heartsease* took sail and the empty land receded, a man seeming no longer a man of flesh and blood but a stick figure, and then no more than a stick, a drawn wavering line on the whiteness of the shore. I see him growing ever smaller and I try to make the leap across the widening gap. How was it there, I ask myself, for him? Seeing what he saw, seeing us go. Such a hard thing it must have been to stand thus far off and have a view so clear, and look back at the rest of humankind.

ACKNOWLEDGEMENTS

I would like to acknowledge a particular debt to two past sailors to the North: to the Icelandic seaman Jon Olafsson, whose narrative of his life (published by the Hakluyt Society) includes an unsubstantiated anecdote about an Englishman's wager, and to the Whitby whaler William Scoresby, whose extraordinary observations are recorded in his *Account of the Arctic Regions*. There was a real Captain Thomas Marmaduke of Hull who made independent whaling voyages to the uncharted east of Svalbard; I have borrowed his name and that of his ship, the *Heartsease*, but all else concerning him is fictional.

I would like to thank Broo and Alexandra for making it such a pleasure getting this published. And David, for the harpoon and much else besides.

NOTE ON THE AUTHOR

Georgina Harding is the author of two works of non-fiction: *Tranquebar: A Season in South India* and *In Another Europe*. This is her first novel.

NOTE ON THE TYPE

The text of this book is set in Bembo. This type was first used in 1495 by the Venetian printer Aldus Manutius for Cardinal Bembo's *De Aetna*, and was cut for Manutius by Francesco Griffo. It was one of the types used by Claude Garamond (1480–1561) as a model for his Romain de L'Université, and so it was the forerunner of what became standard European type for the following two centuries. Its modern form follows the original types and was designed for Monotype in 1929.